CHOICES

A Sussex Crime novella

ISABELLA MUIR

OUTSET PUBLISHING LTD

Published in Great Britain

By Outset Publishing Ltd

First edition published October 2021

ISBN: 9781872889382

www.isabellamuir.com

Cover photo: Bottle Alley, Hastings by Kai Bossom on Unsplash

Cover design: by Christoffer Petersen

CONTENTS

PRAISE FOR THE SUSSEX CRIME NOVELLAS

'A surprising Christmas-themed novella set in a period of great uncertainty.'

'This was a fabulous short story, capturing exactly the excitement of Christmas, and how it must have been at the start of the Second World War. Family is at the heart of the story, with two families whose children are friends.'

'Set during the Second World War this intriguing cozy crime mystery is perfect for dark winter evenings, delivering a satisfying conclusion to a well-written story.'

'...you are taken into the lives of the people who live in this small town near the sea in England during WWII.'

You can discover more about my books and characters on my website. **www.isabellamuir.com**
or follow me on Twitter: **@SussexMysteries**

ONE

WHENEVER ANNABELLE STUBBS WARNED Vera not to venture to the southern end of Sandy Close, Vera asked, 'Why?'. Her mother's response was merely, 'All you need to know is that Y comes before Z'.

Nevertheless, it was the southern end of Sandy Close that Vera simply had to visit, as it was here that Jessica chose to mark out the hopscotch squares. She had drawn them on the ground with pink and white chalk. White for the lines and pink for the numbers.

Vera wanted to know how Jessica had got hold of pink chalk. Once or twice, Vera had seen Mrs Cartwright use coloured chalk. The teacher had drawn a diagram on the blackboard to explain the difference between a triangle and a rectangle. Mrs Cartwright had drawn the diagram in white chalk, adding arrows and words in a colour. If Vera closed her eyes she could see that diagram and, yes, the coloured chalk was pink. Jessica had stolen the chalk from Mrs Cartwright.

That morning, when Jessica walked up to the far end of Sandy Close, Vera was waiting.

'Who's going first?' Jessica said.

'You drew the hopscotch, so you go first.' Authority in Vera's voice, even though Jessica was a year older.

As Jessica stepped forward, putting her right foot into the first square, holding her left leg aloft, Vera called out, 'Did you steal the pink chalk from Mrs Cartwright?'.

Jessica was still for a second or two, looking a bit like an ungainly flamingo, balancing on one leg, before toppling over and landing on her bottom on the ground.

'That's your fault. You made me fall.' She glared at Vera. 'If you don't want to play, that's fine with me. It's a stupid game anyway.'

Without answering Vera's question, Jessica stood up, brushed the dust and chalk from her skirt and headed home.

Home for Vera was Victoria Lodge, a red brick, semi-detached house at the northern end of Rye Road. A little over ten minutes to walk from there to Tamarisk Bay seafront and less than five minutes to the local shops. So far Victoria Lodge remained unaffected by the recent spate of bombings, even though two of the houses half-way along Rye Road were almost flattened three days earlier. The two families had escaped without injury, but their belongings were still in evidence, strewn across the road as if a giant had discarded all his worldly goods in a fit of pique.

Once indoors, Vera changed her outdoor shoes for slippers and looked around the kitchen for something to eat. Breakfast was hours ago. Her sister, Enid, started work at half past eight, even though the shop where she worked didn't open until nine.

'Why?' Vera had asked her sister. 'What do you have to do?'

'Just be there. Make sure we're ready for customers.'

'Why does it take a whole half hour?'

'You and your questions,' was her sister's only response.

Vera grabbed the biscuit jar from the lowest shelf, knowing before she took off the lid that it would be empty. She'd munched through the last handful of broken biscuits yesterday afternoon and the last of the bread had been used for Enid's sandwich. That morning they had porridge for breakfast, with Enid due to bring home a fresh loaf later. But there was a dry crust left over from the day before. She slathered it with some of her mother's homemade blackberry jam. At least it would satisfy whatever was making the gurgling noises deep inside her. Having spread the jam across the bread, she tossed the knife into the sink, vowing to herself to wash it up before her mother emerged from wherever she was. Upstairs changing the beds, perhaps, although that was usually Monday's job. A job that always left her mother red-faced and tired.

Vera hadn't quite decided what she wanted to do when she was grown up. But she was certain about the jobs she didn't want to do. Changing beds for one.

Holding one hand on her stomach to still the rumbling, Vera listened for her mother's footsteps crossing the creaking floorboards above her head. Instead, she heard voices. She strained to pick out the words. Her mother's voice and someone else. Both were speaking quietly.

'I'll have to borrow yours, then,' she heard her mother say.

The reply, when it came, helped her put a name to the voice straight away. Auntie Doris.

'You can choose from two,' Doris said. 'The larger one is smarter, but if you fill it, you'll struggle to carry it. Even when it's empty, I end up dragging it around. It's real leather, you see.'

Then her mother again, whispering so that Vera couldn't catch the words. A few moments later, the conversation stopped, and Annabelle Stubbs and her sister came into the kitchen.

'Oh Vera, look at you. You've jam all round your mouth. You've even dropped some on your jumper. I'll need to get to that straightaway or it'll stain. I never did manage to get the marks out of your other top from the blackberry picking last summer. You'll end up with no clothes to wear at all.'

'Hello Vera.' Auntie Doris nodded a greeting to her niece, stepping towards the back door as though she was loath to get involved in any discussions about stain removal.

'I'll be off.' Doris turned her gaze towards her sister. 'And think about what I said just now. Let me know.'

Vera noticed the exchange of looks between her mother and her aunt and took a breath, ready to ask a question, stopping before a word was uttered. It was the second time she had seen her aunt that day and it was the previous sighting she longed to ask about.

Vera had been walking to Enid's shop. Her sister had rushed out that morning, forgetting to take her lunch. Enid had incurred the wrath of their mother by 'dawdling' over breakfast.

It was the first time Vera had heard the word. She kept rehearsing the sound of it in her head, planning to use it as soon as she could. Not to show off, although she guessed it might look that way.

'Eat up,' their mother had said, in response to Enid's yawns. 'You'd best quit your dawdling or you'll be late for work.'

Enid had responded with a sour look, pushing her plate away, with her porridge barely touched. It was only when the back door slammed closed that Annabelle noticed the greaseproof paper parcel sitting on the kitchen dresser.

'There now, look at that. Your sister has gone and left her lunch. Vera, you'd best run after her with it.'

By the time Vera had changed slippers to shoes, unravelled the knot in her laces before tying them up again, finishing with a double bow, selected a scarf from the hook beside the back door and stepped out into the street, Enid was nowhere to be seen.

There was no need to rush though. The shop didn't open until nine and until then Vera would probably catch Enid in the back storeroom, which was accessed via Pebsham Close.

It was as she turned from Rye Road into the close that she saw her. Auntie Doris. She was at least one hundred yards away, but there was no mistaking her, even from the rear view. Her aunt always wore a distinctive camel coloured coat with a russet scarf wrapped around her shoulders, her dark hair long and loose. And then, the strangest thing. Further away, at the far end of the close was a man sitting on a motorcycle, alongside it a side car. Vera hadn't seen a motorcycle like it before.

The man watched Doris approach, lifting his hand to wave to her. Then, without any hesitation, her aunt ran right up to the man, leaned towards him and kissed him. Vera couldn't believe what she was seeing and, although there was no one close by to hear her, she gasped aloud. Seconds later Auntie Doris climbed into the motorcycle sidecar. Vera retreated around the corner, into a narrow alleyway, where she remained unseen as the kissing couple sped past her.

And now, here was her Auntie Doris standing in front of her.

'Vera, what did I say?' Her mother had been speaking and Vera hadn't heard a single word. 'Take that jumper off so I can get it into soak. Here, let me rub some salt into it first, that might do the trick.'

Half an hour later the jumper was in the sink and Vera was watching her mother make pastry. The mystery of Auntie Doris and the kissing had been put to one side for the moment, now joined by the mystery of the whispered conversation between her mother and her aunt that Vera heard earlier. It was turning into a strange kind of day.

'When will the jam tarts be ready, Mum? We don't have to wait until tea-time, do we? I'm starving.'

'You are not starving. If you were, you would know about it, trust me. And, yes, we will wait until Enid arrives before we touch a single one. Now fetch the pastry cutter and if you promise to be careful, I'll let you cut the bottoms and put the jam in.'

A moment later and the pastry and jam were forgotten as the air raid siren wailed.

'Mummy, make it stop.' Vera shouted above the noise, while clamping her hands over her ears.

Every air raid brought terror, sometimes devastation, sometimes death. How could her mother be so calm? Vera watched as her mother stretched up to the shelf over the sink to take down a saucer and candle and a box of matches. 'Come on, Vera, you know what we have to do now.'

Annabelle took Vera's hand, pulling her in one direction, as Vera pulled against her in a vain attempt to stay in the kitchen.

'You're a big girl now, darling. Ten-year-olds don't behave like babies, do they? You can choose to be scared, or you can choose to be grown up and brave.'

Vera couldn't make any sense of her mother's words; surely you either were scared or you weren't. Nevertheless, she followed her mother into the understairs cupboard. Shoving the coats to one side, they moved deep into the back of the cupboard, as far as headroom would allow. Annabelle set the saucer and candle down on the ground and lit it. They had used the space as an air-raid shelter on several occasions. Annabelle had kitted it out with a packet of Rich Tea biscuits and a flask of orange squash, which she refreshed every day, just in case. She opened the biscuit wrapper, offering the packet towards her daughter. Vera shook her head.

'There now, you were hungry a moment ago, pestering me for jam tarts. Take a biscuit, there's a good girl and we'll share a cup of squash from the flask.'

'I just want the noise to stop.' Vera kept her hands over her ears, squatting down beside her mother, who was sitting on the little wooden stool she had carried in from the garden shed a day or two ago. It seemed to Vera the more she pressed her hands to her ears, the louder the noise from the sirens. It was as if they were inside her head.

'Sing to me, Mummy. Like you did before.'

'Only if you join in,' Annabelle said. The first time they used the shelter, Annabelle had launched into *'We'll meet again,'* telling Vera it was a song that Vera Lynn had been singing on the wireless to cheer the troops. Now they called her the 'Forces Sweetheart'. Vera squeezed out the beginnings of a smile as her mother reached the chorus. The smile seemed to free up Vera's voice too, helping her to join in with the rest of the song, occasionally tripping over the words. But the singing stopped mid chorus when the ground below shook and the wooden slats above their heads creaked and groaned, as if desperate to give way.

'Are we going to die?' Vera gripped onto her mother's leg, stopping her from standing. 'What will happen to Enid if we die?'

Vera leaned forwards, her plait brushing across the candle flame.

'Dear Lord, Vera, look what you've done. Your hair is burning.'

It seemed that terrors could build one upon the other. The smell of singed hair, the darkness that followed when her mother blew out the candle. A tower of fear that stood in front of Vera, blotting out everything that went before.

'What about Enid's shop?' Vera shrieked. 'The bomb might have dropped right there. Enid could be dead, along with Mr and Mrs Thomas and...'

'That's quite enough. We'll have no more talk of dying.' Her mother's voice sharp, almost angry.

Now there was no singing, no talking, only Vera clinging to her mother.

Then Annabelle said, 'Listen, that's the all clear. Let's go back into the kitchen and see if we can finish the baking.'

As Annabelle pushed open the cupboard, a choking cloud of dust greeted them. A fine white powder covered the lino that ran up the centre of the staircase, as if someone had scattered icing sugar.

'Wait right here, Vera,' was her mother's instruction, but an instruction that had to be ignored because as Vera reached the top stair, her mother just ahead of her, she sensed the temperature drop, as though she was walking into a cold store. The sounds of frantic voices and emergency sirens seemed to be coming from Enid's bedroom, rather than the street below.

Vera watched her mother push open the bedroom door to discover no longer a bedroom, but a scene of shattered glass and rubble. The scream had escaped from Vera's mouth before she had time to suppress it.

'Now what did I say? I asked you to stay downstairs.'

Her mother shooed Vera ahead of her along the landing. 'We'll not finish the baking just now. First, you can help me get a bed ready for Enid. She'll share your room tonight and then we'll see what can be done.'

Handing linen from the airing cupboard to Vera, Annabelle arranged cushions and pillows on the floor of Vera's bedroom, adding two sheets and a covering of blankets. Each time Vera opened her mouth to ask a question, her mother raised a finger to her lips.

'Not now, Vera.'

'But Mum...'

'No, Vera. Straighten that corner, will you? You don't want your sister to be cold in the night, do you?'

It was later that afternoon when Enid returned from work and their mother drew her into the pantry, shooing Vera away, that Vera had a chance to confirm her fears. She climbed the stairs, missing the fourth step that always creaked, crept along the landing to Enid's bedroom and opened the door. This time she clamped her hand over her mouth, stifling the noise she knew would give her away. Brick dust and broken glass covered her sister's bed, and sitting on top of the bedcovers, which no longer resembled bedcovers, was a large boulder. The chilly evening air blew in freely. With barely a few fragments of window glass left embedded around the wooden frame, there was no protection from the elements. Looking out through a broken pane Vera examined the street below for clues as to how the boulder had ended up on her sister's bed. The blast from the bomb had created a crater, midway between the row of houses opposite and Victoria Lodge, the Stubbs' family home. The force from the blast had shattered the windows, with brick and masonry showering down from nearby buildings, forcing the boulder up, like a bouncing ball, leaving it to land on Enid's bed.

'Vera, downstairs now.' Her mother's voice, impatient, irritable. Enid stood behind their mother, looking over her shoulder at her books, which were no longer stacked neatly on her bedside table, but jumbled in a pile on the floor.

'If Enid had been in bed, the boulder would have killed her,' Vera said. It was a statement of fact. A fact Vera wanted acknowledging as she looked from her sister to her mother.

'She would never have been in her bed, though, would she?' Annabelle said. 'Because if Enid had been at home, we would all have been safe in the understairs cupboard, wouldn't we? Now come and wash your hands and we'll have tea. Tomorrow I'll get us some help to clear the mess and fix the window.'

Her mother would sort it out. It was a reassurance of sorts. But much more reassurance was needed if Vera was to sleep that night.

Usually, an hour or so passed between Vera's bedtime and her sister's. This time Vera was determined to stay awake for as long as was necessary until Enid crept into the bedroom.

'I'm not asleep,' Vera said.

'And you're not in your bed.'

'It's better if you sleep in my bed. You have work tomorrow.'

'Thanks, sis.' Enid undressed, tossing her clothes over the iron bedstead at the foot of the bed before climbing in and tugging the blankets up under her chin. 'We need to ask Mum if there are any more blankets in the loft. Are you okay?'

Vera didn't respond. She held two secrets, both involving Auntie Doris, but one would need to remain secret for now, even from her sister.

'Auntie Doris was here today talking with Mum. Well, mostly they were whispering.' Vera paused.

'How do you mean?'

'Enid, what sort of thing might be heavy even when it's empty and when it's full it's heavier still? Oh, and maybe made of leather.'

'Enough of your riddles now, you should be asleep. It's late.'

'Really though, Enid. I need to know.'

'A bag, I suppose. Or a suitcase. Now go to sleep and don't wake me too early tomorrow.'

'Why would Mum want to borrow a bag or a suitcase from Auntie Doris?'

'How should I know?'

So many minutes passed without another word from Enid, Vera feared her sister had fallen asleep.

'Enid, do you think Mum is planning to go away? If she leaves us, I'll probably die.'

'What is it with you and your fixation with dying? You've got yourself all stirred up because of the air raid and the bomb blast. Look, Mum is fine, and so are we. A broken window and some mess to clear is not the end of the world. Try to think of something nice and you'll soon drop off to sleep.'

'But it's only Mum who keeps me safe. She sings to me when we're in the shelter together. She makes everything alright. If she's not here to look after us, what will happen?'

'Ssh now. Try counting sheep.'

'Enid.'

'What is it now?'

'I wish Dad was here.'

TWO

MATTHEW STUBBS JOINED THE RAF as soon as the
rumblings of war became ever more serious. On the day he left,
Vera pleaded with her mother for one of the small photos that
usually sat on the mantlepiece beside the carriage clock.

'Mind you look after it now,' her mother warned.

And now, every night before closing her eyes, Vera kissed her
father's photograph. In the photo Matthew Stubbs smiles
directly at the camera. An open-necked shirt, a jumper slung
around his shoulders and one hand raised with a 'thumbs up'
sign. The photo helped Vera remember her father's face, but she
needed no help to remember his smell. Shaving soap and
Everton mints. She never tired of hearing his account of the day
the photo was taken.

'Everton had just won. Scored the winning goal in the final
minute. I came straight home from the match, took off my tie
and jumper and your mum used the camera we'd bought only
the week before. It was the first photo she'd ever taken.'

Arnold went on to give Vera a kick-by-kick account of the
game. Vera listened, understanding very little, but revelling in
the joy she detected in her father's voice as he described the
'nifty passes', the 'clever tackles' and finally the winning goal. 'A
masterpiece, it was. Dixie Dean is just about the greatest goal

scorer the game has known,' he said. 'The goalie didn't stand a chance.'

And, as if to honour his team, every Saturday Arnold took Vera to the corner shop, giving her the money to buy a few pennies' worth of Everton mints. They walked down to Bottle Alley, the covered walkway below the seafront and sitting on one of the concrete seats, gazing out to sea, Matthew unwrapped two Everton mints, giving one to Vera, before popping one into his mouth. They enjoyed the sweets in silence. Then, once there was nothing left to suck or chew, just the tang of mint flavour remaining, Arnold recounted the story of the Everton mint and how it came to have its black and white stripes.

'It was all down to old Mother Noblett and her sweet shop. The Everton football fans passed her shop on the way to the match, so she got to thinking if she made a sweet and called it after the Everton team then she would have plenty of customers for it.'

'Why was it black and white?'

'Because that was the colour of the team's football strip.'

'Why is it called a strip?'

There was so much Vera didn't understand about the story. In fact, most of her father's stories left her with questions. But the joy was in the listening and watching his eyes light up and his hands fly around as he described the moments that gave him such pleasure. He told her about the time Uncle Bill was asked to try out for the Everton football team. It was strange though because Uncle Bill had never mentioned it, neither had Auntie Doris. So maybe it hadn't happened at all. No matter.

Vera had made a pledge to herself. Even if they stopped sweet rationing this very day, she wouldn't sit on their favourite bench or enjoy a single Everton mint until her father was sitting beside her.

Over the next few days there was a list of jobs to be tackled. Mr Tester called in with his measuring tape and Enid's bedroom window was boarded up. Before that, Vera and Enid helped their mother clear the rubble, strip the bed and empty the chest of drawers. Every item of clothing, every piece of bed linen, had to be rinsed first and then washed. There was a waiting list of items for the washing line that stretched across their back garden. No sooner was one load dry than the next had to be pegged out. Annabelle told her daughters her prayers for fine weather had been answered. The blankets were more of a problem. All that could be done was to hang them double over the line and beat them with the broom to chase away as much of the dust as possible. Two neighbours helped to drag the mattress outside, and Vera watched her mother strike it again and again, first with the broom and then a hand brush. There seemed to be little sense to all the beating as the dust came out in clouds and landed on the washing. A relentless cycle of trying to make do, being repeated in many of the houses and gardens along Rye Road.

Now and then residents paused from their chores, gathering in small groups to agree on how lucky they were, how it could have been much, much worse. At least no one had been injured or died. This time. There was enough news of death among their men who had left to fight, many never to return.

Four days after the bomb blast, the clean-up operation was complete. It seemed there was no plan to put new glass into the bedroom window. A fact that bothered Vera to such an extent, she couldn't hold back.

The family was at breakfast. It was the first day of the new school term, although starting back on a Friday seemed an odd thing to Vera. One day only, and then the weekend. Regardless, she was excited about seeing her teacher again. She had written a report of recent events in her exercise book and was certain if Mrs Cartwright read it, she would award Vera a gold star. The kudos of being top of the class for reading and writing was something Vera was keen to hang on to. Her dad would be proud. Her mum too, although it was hard to be sure. But it wasn't easy writing really good stories when she was sleeping on the floor of her bedroom, with her sister still sleeping in Vera's bed.

'When will Enid move back into her bedroom?' Vera posed the question as she stretched her arm across the table to take the last slice of bread, almost knocking over the milk jug in the process.

'How many pieces have you had already?' Annabelle asked, taking the bread from Vera's hand and putting it back on the bread board. 'You should ask everyone else first before taking the last piece. It's manners, Vera. Remember to mind your manners.'

'What's the answer, Mum?'

'The answer to what? Vera, you and your questions, they quite make my head swirl. Now, wash your hands and face, brush your teeth, and get your satchel ready. Enid is going to walk you to school this morning.'

Annabelle cleared away the crockery, putting the last slice of bread back into the bread bin. The bread would remain uneaten, and Vera's question would remain unanswered.

The first day back at school was full of organisation and catching up for Mrs Cartwright, leaving her no time in the school day to read Vera's story.

'I'll take it home tonight and read it then. How about that?' Mrs Cartwright said, in response to Vera's repeated attempts to push the exercise book into her hand.

At half past three the school bell rang for the end of lessons. Jessica had kept away from Vera all through dinner break and playtime. It seemed she was still upset at being called a thief. Well, there was nothing Vera could do about that right now, so without a backward glance, as soon as Mrs Cartwright rang the bell, Vera ran outside. Her gaze swept across the faces of the mothers standing around the edge of the playground. Vera wanted to tell her mother that Mrs Cartwright was treating the story about the bombing with special consideration. She was taking it home with her. She wasn't taking any other stories home. At least that's what it sounded like. But Annabelle Stubbs was clearly running late. Vera moved to one corner of the playground, watching her friends leave. Five or ten minutes passed. Vera didn't have a watch so she couldn't be sure, but it felt like an age. She prepared a list of possibilities in her mind. There had been no air raids during the day, so her mother couldn't have been caught in a blast. Perhaps she had tried to rearrange the furniture in Enid's bedroom and had fallen and hurt her back. Annabelle had fallen once before and after that Vera often saw her mum rubbing her lower back. She heard the word 'lumbago' being mentioned. She looked it up in the dictionary at school.

'Still here, Vera? Doesn't your mother usually collect you?' Mrs Cartwright stood in front of Vera, stooping slightly to catch the girl's eye.

And then a shout.

'Vera. There you are.' Auntie Doris crossed the playground, taking Vera's hand a little too roughly, causing the child to pull away.

'Where's Mum?' Vera directed her question more at Mrs Cartwright than at her aunt.

'You and Enid are coming to stay with me for a while. Won't that be nice?' It seemed to Vera that Auntie Doris was convincing herself as much as her niece.

'Well now, Vera. There's a treat for you. Off you go now and I'll see you on Monday.' Mrs Cartwright turned and, without hesitation, walked back into the school.

Vera fell into step behind her aunt, breaking any silence before it began by asking, 'Why isn't Mum here?'

'You're to come and stay with me, at my house. It'll be like a holiday for you and your sister.'

'Why?'

'Don't be difficult, Vera.'

'Has Mum fallen over again?'

'Fallen over? No, not at all. You are a funny thing, always asking questions. Your mother has gone to visit your father, that's all. She didn't want to tell you before because she knew you'd make a fuss.'

'I want to see Dad too. Why didn't she take us?'

'Your father is doing dangerous things. Flying planes into battle and all sorts. He can't be worrying about you two now, can he? Not when there's a war to fight.'

It seemed to Vera that every answer led to more questions. A never-ending cycle and an endless challenge, trying to grasp the intentions of the adults around her. She had learned that adults soon tired of her questions and instead of providing unhelpful answers, they provided no response at all.

Doris Frith lived three streets away from Vera's house. She and her husband, Bill, had moved into a two-bedroom cottage when they first married, which was the year before Vera was born. Vera and Enid had visited a handful of times, and after their last visit, Vera had written in her diary. 'Auntie Doris's house is spiky and cold.' No one read her diary, at least she didn't think they did, because she guessed her mum would be cross about some of the things Vera had said about her Auntie Doris.

It wasn't just that the house had a damp chill about it, there was an odd smell too. Vera smelled it again as Doris turned the front door key and stood to one side gesturing to Vera to step onto the door mat.

'Stop right there and take your shoes off. Your satchel can go here, look.' Doris pointed at a coat stand that had two hooks, one set too high for Vera to reach, another lower down but still a stretch. Vera hung the strap of her satchel over the lower hook, then bent down to untie her shoelaces.

'You can hang your jumper up too if you like.'

'No, you're alright. I mean, no, thank you, Auntie.'

'Come and help me get tea ready.'

The smell was stronger in the kitchen, reminding Vera of bleach and wax polish. It was making her feel queasy.

'What about Enid?'

'Your sister finishes work at five thirty. You know that.'

'How will she know where to go?'

'Your mother told her the plan. She'll know to come here.'

'Why?'

'There you go again with your questions.'

'Why did she tell Enid and she didn't tell me?'

No response was forthcoming. Vera would have to wait for her sister's arrival for her questions to be answered.

THREE

AS IT TURNED OUT there was no time to question Enid when she arrived back from the shop. Both girls were set tasks. They were to wash their hands and face, lay the table, put their few belongings into the solitary chest of drawers in the guest bedroom. Enid had arrived with a shopping bag with toothbrushes for both of them, pyjamas, a change of underwear and socks and Vera's favourite teddy, which she still wouldn't be parted from, despite being told that at the age of ten she was too grown up for such things.

They were to share a double bed. Vera pulled Bear from the bag and set him between the two pillows, then picked him up again, wrapping him in the jacket of her pyjamas and laying him on the left side of the bed.

'Will you sleep next to the window?' Vera said to her sister.

'You're scared about another bomb blast, aren't you? Well, don't be. You know what they say about lightning?'

The expression on Vera's face confirmed to Enid that she had said the wrong thing.

'How long will we have to stay here?' Vera kept her voice low, but not quite a whisper.

And then their aunt was calling them to the dining room. 'Don't dilly dally up there. I've made rock cakes and they're best eaten warm.'

The last time Enid and Vera had visited their aunt, Uncle Bill sat at the head of the table and liked three sugars in his tea. Vera couldn't remember much else about him, except for his throaty laugh and puffed-out cheeks, a fascinating mix of patches of red, threaded through with fine blue lines.

Doris passed the plate of rock cakes to Enid, after taking one herself. Enid took two, cutting one and sliding it onto Vera's plate. It crumbled into several pieces, crumbs scattering onto the tablecloth. Doris made a huffing sound as though irritated, either at the way the cakes had turned out, or at the mess the girls were making on the starched linen cloth.

'We don't have fire drills anymore,' Vera said, licking her fingers before trying to gather up some of the cake crumbs. 'At school. We used to have them every Friday, but now we have air raid drills. We all have to pretend the siren is sounding and follow Mrs Cartwright out to the shelter. If anyone runs, they get told off.'

'Yes, well,' Doris said.

'And they've taken the railings away from the playground. Some men came with a big truck at the end of last term and pulled them out of the ground. Mrs Cartwright said to keep away from the windows when we tried to watch.'

'It's all part of the war effort,' Doris said.

'What do the soldiers want our railings for? Are they going to build a big barricade to keep the Germans out?'

'They melt them down,' Enid said.

'Is Uncle Bill with Dad?' Vera asked. 'Are they both shooting at people?'

'Your uncle is a soldier. Your dad is a pilot. But let's have no more talk of fighting. Now eat up, there are chores to do when you're finished.'

Later, when the tea things were washed and dried, Vera and Enid learned which cupboards held the crockery and how to stack the plates in order of size.

'It's best to have a system,' Doris said. 'That way we make sure nothing gets chipped. I can't be doing with chipped plates.'

Vera thought about the crockery at home, how she always knew which was her plate because of the two chipped areas next to each other. Thinking about it now, it felt as though she missed that plate more than anything.

They spent the early evening in the front room. Doris pulled out a small wicker basket from behind her armchair.

'Our soldiers need socks,' she said, moving the knitting needles in such a way Vera imagined the needles were knives or guns, ready to stab or shoot the enemy.

'Vera, choose a book from the shelf over there and read aloud to us,' Doris said, without looking up from her knitting.

The sisters exchanged a sideways glance. The only time Vera had to read aloud was in the classroom. At home she read to herself at bedtime, while Enid like to flick through magazines.

'Do I have to?' Vera asked, moving over to the bookshelves to determine whether there was anything there that might keep three people entertained.

'How about this?' Doris slid out a small hard-backed book, handing it to Vera. 'It was a favourite of your mother and I when we were your age.'

Vera stared at the book's title. *The Secret Garden*. She tried to imagine her mother and Auntie Doris sitting together, being read to by their father or mother. She realised she couldn't form a picture.

Vera opened the book to the first chapter and started to read. All the while she was reading, her aunt's repetitive movements distracted her. Each time Doris reached the end of a row of knitting, she set the needles down on her lap and ran her hand over her hair, which she wore long and loose.

'What are you staring at, Vera? Why have you stopped reading?' Doris said.

'Why does Mum always wear a scarf on her head?'

'How should I know?'

'Why don't you wear a scarf, Auntie?'

'Someone told me recently how my hair resembles black velvet.' Doris seemed to have fallen into a reverie, stroking her hair and staring into the embers of the fire.

Only when both girls giggled did she refocus.

'How old was Mum when you used to read together?' Vera asked.

'What does it matter?' Doris threw her knitting down, the needles landing with a clatter on the edge of the hearth. 'You'd best both go up to bed together tonight.'

'But it's not my bedtime yet,' Enid said.

'Make sure you brush your teeth. You can get undressed down here by the fire, if you like.' Doris stood and when neither girl moved, she clapped her hands. 'Chop, chop, let's be quick about it, shall we? And if you behave yourselves, then in the morning we can have bread and dripping. We'll light the fire early and toast it right here.'

Enid led the way to the bathroom, with Vera following behind. Once the door was pulled closed, Vera stood in front of the mirror and stuck her tongue out. 'I don't like Auntie Doris. I don't believe she's really Mum's sister and I don't even like toast and dripping.'

'Ssh, Vera, she'll hear you. She might be standing outside the door right now.'

'Well, I'm not staying here. I'll go home and wait for Mum to come back.'

'Don't be silly. You can't live in the house on your own. Besides, what about me? You can't leave me here with the dragon.'

Vera started giggling before putting her hands across her mouth, which made her sister giggle even more.

'Why has Mum gone away?' Vera asked once the giggling had subsided. 'Auntie Doris said she'd told you about it.'

Enid shrugged. 'She just said she was going to see Dad.'

'But how long for? When will she come back?'

'She's written us a letter. I'll read it to you later.'

Doris interrupted the conversation by knocking on the door. 'Are you done in there? I hope you haven't made a mess.'

Without waiting for a reply, Doris opened the door and shooed both girls through to the bedroom. 'Now get your night things and come down to the front room.'

Ten minutes later, they escaped back to the bedroom, after instructions from their aunt to fold their clothes neatly and a warning they should be ready for an early start in the morning.

Vera pulled back the blanket and slid into bed, but swiftly jumped out again.

'Now what?' Enid said. 'You haven't found a spider in there, have you?'

'It's freezing. Mum always puts a brick in to warm it.'

'Yes, well, we're not at home now, so we'll have to put up with it. Put your socks back on, then at least I won't have to have your icy toes touching me.'

'Will you show me the letter Mum wrote us?'

Enid took a single sheet of paper out from her skirt pocket, before folding her skirt again and setting it on top of her sister's clothes.

'I'll read it to you.'

'Dearest Enid and Vera

I'm going away for a little while to see your dad. He's coming up for a spot of leave but there's no time for him to come back to us, so I need to go to him.

Please be good for your Auntie Doris. I love you both very much.

Your mum.'

'She doesn't say for how long.' Vera said, her bottom lip wobbling, despite her attempts to control it.

'Well, maybe she doesn't know.'

'Do you think she's gone for ever? Grown ups don't always tell the truth, you know.'

'You're always imagining the worst possible thing. Look, she'll be back in no time, you'll see.'

'Will Auntie Doris have to adopt us if Mum doesn't come back? Or will we have to live in Canada? Sarah Sharp at school, both her parents are dead, and she's being sent to Canada. I heard Mrs Cartwright talking about it. I don't want to go to Canada.'

Vera snuggled up to her sister, pressing her head against Enid's shoulder.

'I don't like it here.'

'Ssh now. Close your eyes and try to sleep.'

But sleep wasn't going to settle either of the girls for a while yet. Footsteps on the stairs and the sound of a door opening suggested something worth investigating.

'Auntie Doris can't be coming to bed already, can she?' Vera asked her sister. 'Be very quiet, I'm going to take a look.' Vera stepped into her slippers, crept out of the room and along the landing, holding her breath for fear of discovery.

Doris's bedroom was a little further down the landing, the other side of the bathroom. At least if Vera got caught, she could pretend she was going to the toilet. Her aunt's door was open, giving Vera a clear view of Doris sitting in front of her dressing-table mirror brushing her hair. Vera watched as Doris lifted the silver-backed hairbrush to the crown of her head, pulling it firmly down across her thick locks, then repeating the action over and over. After several minutes Doris laid the brush down and slid open a little drawer to one side of the dressing table. Vera stood transfixed as her aunt rubbed her lips with what looked like beetroot juice, moving her face close to the mirror, puckering her lips into a pout. Doris pinched her cheeks, making them blush a fiery red. Then Vera sensed an overwhelming need to sneeze. Clamping her hand over her nose and mouth she tiptoed back to her bedroom to find Enid sitting up in bed, waiting for a full report.

She's getting all dolled up,' Vera said. 'There's no way she's going to bed.' Perhaps now was the moment to tell Enid what she knew, about her aunt kissing a stranger. 'Is Auntie Doris going to leave us? What's if there's an air raid?'

Enid shrugged, moving over to the window. 'We'll be able to see if she goes out. Come and watch with me, turn the light out while I open the blackout curtains. If the warden sees even a chink of light, we'll be for it.'

The strict rules governing blackouts and night-time curfews meant people rarely ventured onto the streets at night without a justifiable reason. The moonlight cast patchy shadows on the street below. The girls watched for several moments. Vera grabbed Enid's hand.

'Look, down there.' Vera pointed at the corner of the road, about six houses down. 'I just saw something move.'

'Something or someone?'

'There's someone coming up the street. Enid, it's a man, he's coming right up to the house.'

Vera's voice was no longer a whisper.

Then everything happened at once. A rattling of the front door handle, the sound of Doris's footsteps running downstairs, with both girls following close behind. Vera watched as her aunt picked up the fire poker, holding it aloft before slowly sliding back the chain on the front door.

'Who's there?' Doris called out. 'Make yourself known right now.'

'Maybe it's a Nazi come to murder us in our beds,' Vera offered up to anyone taking notice. But neither Doris nor Enid was listening to Vera, both had their attention focused on the response from the stranger standing on the front doorstep.

'Doris, it's me – Bill. Let me in, will you?' Uncle Bill arriving home without warning. This time it wasn't only Vera who had questions.

FOUR

THERE WAS NO TOASTED bread and dripping the next morning for breakfast and Uncle Bill seemed to have lost his hearty laugh. Doris's face looked pale by comparison with the evening before. Her hair was pulled back and twisted into a bun, with plenty of hair grips keeping it in place. Vera wanted to ask Uncle Bill if he preferred his wife's hair long and loose, like 'black velvet', or whether she had pinned it out of the way at his request. But Bill's sour expression deterred her from asking any questions at all.

The girls didn't need to be asked to clear away the breakfast things. Being on their own in the kitchen to wash and dry and put away was preferable to sitting in silence around the dining table.

'They don't seem very pleased to see each other,' Vera whispered to her sister, once the kitchen door was firmly shut.

'Maybe he's upset she nearly hit him with the fire iron.'

The memory of her aunt's expression the evening before, when her husband stepped into the hallway made Vera giggle.

'If she didn't know he was coming home, why was she getting all dolled up?' Enid asked.

Vera might have had the answer, but instead she shrugged. 'Maybe she was practising.'

A few minutes later Auntie Doris appeared at the kitchen door holding out a piece of paper.

'I've got an errand for you both. Take this note to Mr Kirby at the newsagent's. Ask him to put it in the window. I'm sick and tired of finding mice droppings in the larder. A cat will soon see them off. Once you're done there go to the greengrocer's. I've heard he's taken in a crate of oranges. See if you can't get two or three. Here's the money, but mind you bring back the change.'

For the whole of the short walk to the newsagent's Vera alternated between hopping and skipping. It was a reminder she hadn't played hopscotch with Jessica for days. She could make an excuse, offer to do some shopping for her aunt and meet up with Jessica. But then she would have to call at Jessica's house and Jessica's mother would find out what they were doing and the whole plan would be ruined before it had even begun. Nevertheless, if Auntie Doris didn't know that Sandy Close was out of bounds there was still a chance Vera could go there without being told off.

Vera had two theories as to why the place was out of bounds. It could be that someone dangerous lived in Roebuck House, the old house at the very end of the road, maybe a bank robber, even a murderer. She had read about such things in her dad's newspaper. The other possibility, and the one that Vera favoured, was that Roebuck House was haunted. Perhaps a murder had taken place in one of the rooms and the victim's spirit was destined never to leave the place.

Being engrossed in these thoughts resulted in Vera bumping into her sister, who had stopped outside the newsagent's and was pointing at the placard announcing the day's headline.

'RAF suffers losses in northern France.'

Vera read the words aloud, repeating them slowly, her voice increasing in volume until she shrieked the final word.

'Dad,' she said.

'We don't know that,' Enid said, holding her sister by the shoulders, gently turning her away so she was no longer facing the placard. Vera struggled from her sister's grip and picked up a newspaper from the stack beside the placard. Before she had a chance to open the broadsheet to read the article Mr Kirby emerged from the shop.

'I'll have the money for that newspaper before you start reading it, young lady.' He held his hand out expectantly.

'We've only got money for oranges.'

'Then you'd best put it back where you found it and hope you've not creased it too much.' His hands were on his hips, his gaze shifting from Vera to Enid and back again.

'I need to read it though,' Vera persisted. 'It could be about my dad. He's an RAF pilot.'

'You'd better come back with some money then, hadn't you?'

It was a standoff that couldn't be resolved. Vera was being pulled away, Enid tugging at her arm.

'Come on, we'd best get in the queue for the oranges, or they'll all be gone.'

For the forty-five minutes the sisters stood in the queue at the greengrocer's Vera wouldn't let the subject drop. Every possibility was dissected, every fear explored.

'If Dad is dead and Mum is too sad to come home, we might still have to go to Canada to live, like Sarah Sharp,' Vera said.

'You're adding two and two and making them add up to seven.'

'What does that mean?'

'That you're jumping to conclusions. We don't even know if Dad was flying that day. He and Mum are probably having a fine time, eating a bag of chips on Brighton seafront.'

'But what if they're not?'

'That's enough, Vera. Stop, will you?'

They had reached the head of the queue. The greengrocer was shaking his head. 'If you're here for oranges, I've just sold the last of them.'

'Now we'll be for it. We should have come here first. Auntie Doris will have our guts for garters.' Enid took her sister's hand and pulled her in the direction of home, or at least the place they were to call home for now. With the petrol rationing in force so few cars were on the road, that there was no need to look both ways before crossing. Suddenly, out of nowhere, a motorcycle turned the corner, heading straight towards the sisters.

'Watch out.' A man's voice loud above the throaty noise of the engine.

Enid grabbed Vera and together they fell onto the far side of the road, the motorcycle screeching to a halt yards away. The motorcyclist approached, removing his cycle helmet, as well as the scarf he had wrapped across his mouth, revealing his swarthy features. Thick eyebrows, a full beard and long sideboards and bronzed skin, giving him the look of a foreigner.

'You should look where you're going. I could have killed you.'

'You should look where you're going,' Vera said.

'Mind your manners, little girl. Hasn't anyone told you to respect your elders.'

'I'm very sorry, sir,' Enid said. 'Come on, Vera, we need to go.'

'So you should be,' the man said, wagging a finger at Vera.

They were standing now, Vera intent on inspecting the damage inflicted by the fall. A grazed knee that was bleeding a little, mud on her skirt and what looked like engine oil across the top of one of her socks.

'He's the one who should be sorry,' Vera said, once they were out of earshot. She opened her mouth again, ready to tell her sister the whole story, about what she had seen going on just days ago between her aunt and this man. It was a scandal. It seemed almost certain that this swarthy stranger was her aunt's fancy man. No wonder Uncle Bill had been so grumpy that morning.

But she guessed what her sister would say. Enid would tell Vera that she was imagining it, or that she was making up stories, all because Vera didn't want to stay at Auntie Doris's house. No, the secret must remain a secret until she had gathered more evidence.

Once back at their aunt's house there was no sensible order to the explanations offered by Enid when confronted by a barrage of questions. Her attempts to explain why their clothes were in such disarray, why they had returned without oranges and why Vera's knee was bleeding, tumbled out in a breathless jumble. When questioned about the 'Cat wanted' notice that should have been handed over to the newsagent, all Enid could do was hand the note back to her aunt and apologise.

'We forgot,' she said.

'How did you forget? You went out for two things and haven't managed to achieve either.' Doris's voice rose to a higher pitch the more irritated she became.

'Because Dad might be dead,' Vera said. It was the first thing she had contributed to the conversation and her statement hung in the air as Doris looked first at Enid and then at Vera.

'I've never known a child like it.' Doris threw her hands in the air. 'A fixation with death, that's what it is. And it's unhealthy if you ask me. Now, both of you go upstairs, change out of those grubby clothes, wash the grit and blood off that knee, Vera, and mind you don't get any of it on my towels.'

Vera's mind was made up, there was nothing else for it. She couldn't stay in her aunt's house a moment longer, but she couldn't share her plan with her sister because Enid would be certain to stop her.

Vera managed to persuade her aunt that she was old enough and responsible enough to return to the paper shop to place the advert for the cat.

'Straight there and straight back, mind,' her aunt warned.

'I should go with her, Auntie,' Enid said, but she had been set the task of washing the mud and grease-spattered clothes.

'She's ten years old. She's big enough to run errands on her own.'

Vera took nothing with her. Victoria Lodge would be her base while she gathered all the evidence she needed. There was a lot to sort out. First to establish the truth about her father. Her mother must have heard about the RAF casualties and gone to see for herself if Vera's father was among them. Then there was the motorcycle man to find out about. She would watch out for him, maybe follow him.

The spare key for Victoria Lodge was where it always was, under the flowerpot on the front step. Unlocking the front door and stepping inside, the stillness was cold and unwelcoming. The curtains were drawn, shutting out even a sliver of light. They would have to remain closed if Vera was to go undetected.

She really wanted to return to the newsagent to buy the paper so she could read the front-page article about the RAF plane. But there had been no opportunity to pinch the coppers she needed to cover the price of the newspaper. Her aunt hadn't trusted her enough to give her the money for the advert, telling her to explain to Mr Kirby that Mrs Frith would call in and pay before the end of the week.

No, Vera's best course of action was to fetch some money from the Brooke Bond tea caddy that her mother kept at the back of the cupboard under the sink. She had seen her mother put money in there often enough. She could take a few pennies from the tin and fetch the paper later, although that would be risky if Auntie Doris had sent out a search party.

The thought of uniformed policemen out looking for her gave Vera a funny feeling, as if she was in the centre of her own adventure story. And when she was excited, she needed to eat. She would prepare herself a sandwich and then make a plan.

She pulled open the pantry door, surveying the contents of the shelves. A tin of corned beef, a bag of flour, some jars of lentils and pearl barley. Below was a bottle of camp coffee, a packet of dried egg and a big jar of salt. Aside from the corned beef there was nothing that could stave off the hunger pangs, which were now distracting her from concentrating on anything beyond food.

She took the corned beef from the shelf, moving back into the kitchen, before taking the tiny key from the side of the tin. She had seen her mother open a corned beef tin on many occasions, but she had never been allowed to try it herself. There was a knack to it, she was certain. Prising open the small flap of metal she looped the key over it, trying first one way up before turning the key a full 180 degrees. Another pair of hands was what she really needed, but her own grit and determination would have to do. Concentrating on pushing as much force into her fingers as she could muster, she made the key turn once.

'Hooray.' Despite there being no one around to hear her, she could not help but exclaim her pleasure.

Steady force was needed as she continued, the thin band of metal unwinding to reveal the corned beef, the smell of it wafting towards her, making her mouth water. She had reached the end. Negotiating the corners of the tin had taken concentration but now she needed to ease open the top part of the tin to shake the block of meat out onto the plate she had already taken from the dresser. But she wasn't careful enough. Her hand caught the sharp steel edge. At first there was no pain, only a thin red line of blood seeping out from the top of her thumb. She watched for a second with fascination as the blood dripped onto the plate. It was as though her senses needed time to catch up, because then the pain kicked in, travelling from her thumb up her arm into her shoulder. A fiery burst of pain that blocked her thoughts. All hunger pangs gone in an instant.

The last time she hurt herself she had been cutting out pictures of famous people from one of her mother's magazines. Her mother was angry with her, and Vera couldn't decide if it was because the blood had fallen onto the settee, or because she had destroyed the magazine without asking. On that occasion her mother had taken hold of Vera's hand, tugging her towards the kitchen, letting the cold tap run over the cut. The water was so cold that after a while there was no pain, in fact, her whole hand was numb.

That was the answer. Holding her hand under the running water staved off the pain, but as soon as she turned off the tap the blood appeared again in a steady stream. Perhaps there were plasters somewhere, or a bandage, but how could she apply either when only one hand was working properly. Instead, she grabbed the tea towel from the hook beside the stove and wrapped it as tight as she could around her hand. Then she sat at the kitchen table and stared at the covered-up thumb, waiting for the blood to appear, turning the creamy white of the Irish linen tea towel into a pale pink and then a dark red. She wondered how much blood she needed to lose before she collapsed. How long would it be before someone found her? Would her mother feel guilty for having abandoned her? Would Auntie Doris regret having shouted at her?

The pain subsided a little, leaving the hunger to return. A corned beef sandwich would have been perfect, but a sandwich needed bread and a peek inside the bread bin confirmed her fears. No bread, not even a dry crust. Her mother must have thrown the last of it away before she left. Vera stared at the block of corned beef, which was now spattered with her blood. Hardly appetising. She could cut a slice off and eat it just like that, without any bread. But there was something else that would fill the void. The supply of biscuits her mother kept in the emergency store in the understairs cupboard. With half the packet munched through and barely digested, Vera settled back at the kitchen table to figure out her next move.

She didn't have long. Taking money from the Brooke Bond tea tin and returning to the paper shop was a bad plan, after all. She was bound to be caught, her aunt and her sister would come looking for her and Mr Kirby's newsagent's would be the first place they'd think of. She needed a better plan. More than that she had to enlist help. Figuring out the truth about her father, getting to the facts about her mother's disappearance, and solving the mystery of any possible relationship between 'motorcycle man' and her Auntie Doris, was all too much to tackle on her own. Jessica Chandler. She was sure to want to help. She had already shown Vera she didn't care what people thought of her; after all Jessica had stolen the pink chalk and chosen to draw the hopscotch in the very place they had been told not to play. But the last time Vera had spoken to Jesssica she had accused her of being a thief. They hadn't parted as friends. Vera had to find a way to make up and get her back onside. And she would have to do it quickly if any of this was going to turn out well.

FIVE

THE TELEPHONE BOX AT the corner of South Street and Winchester Street provided the perfect hiding place for Vera as she waited for Jessica to appear. She didn't have to wait long. With a clear view of the side alley that led to Jessica's back door, she saw her friend emerge, a wicker basket over one arm, calling out, 'I won't be long,' to her mother as the door closed behind her.

With the tea towel still wrapped tightly around her hand, Vera grabbed Jessica's arm, just as she passed by the phone box.

'Vera, what are you doing here?'

'I need your help.' Vera chose to whisper, lending the necessary stealth to the request.

'What's the matter with your hand?'

Vera shrugged off the question.

'Anyway,' Jessica continued. 'Why should I help you? The last time we spoke you called me a thief.'

'I'm sorry about that. But I really need your help. It's very complicated and I can't sort it out on my own.'

'Come on, follow me.' No more words were exchanged until the two girls were around the corner from Jessica's house. A bus shelter provided a useful spot for them to sit unnoticed and converse unheard.

'My dad might be dead.' Vera opened the conversation.

'Has your mum had a telegram?'

'Why? Is that what they do? Is that how they tell you when someone has been killed?'

'Vivienne Salter. She's in Mrs Fawcett's class. Her mum got a telegram. They came and took Vivienne out of school. She hasn't been back since.'

Vera ran through the sequence of events. Her mother disappearing without a word, with no more than a brief conversation with Enid and a letter.

'Did the letter say your dad was dead?'

'No. She wrote she was going to see him. But everyone knows that grown-ups lie.'

'I'm not sure it's a lie if it's to stop someone being upset.'

'What is it then?'

'Why do you want my help, anyway? I'm really sorry if your dad is dead, but there's not much I can do about it.'

'We've had to go live with Auntie Doris.'

'Don't you like her?'

Vera shrugged. 'Then there's a man. He's got a motorcycle with a side car. I know a big secret about him and Auntie Doris. And now Uncle Bill has come home on leave.'

'Did he catch them kissing?' Vera could tell from her friend's tone that Jessica found her report as thrilling as watching a film at the cinema. Intrigue, suspense, romance.

'It's not just about the kissing, don't you see?' Vera sensed her friend hadn't grasped the implications of her revelations. 'You know what happened to Olive Dart, don't you? Her dad came home on leave to find his wife had gotten friendly with the delivery chap from the butcher's. Her dad threw them out of the house, and they had to move in with Olive's grandmother and apparently old Mrs Deal refused to speak to either of them. She called Olive's mum a "brazen hussy".' Vera said the words slowly for emphasis.

'So, what do you think we should do?' Jessica said.

'We'll have to track down motorcycle man and follow him. If we see him and Auntie Doris together, we'll know for certain.'

'Then what?'

'We can warn him off. We'll catch him on his own and tell him to go away, and if he doesn't, we'll tell Uncle Bill.'

'Why would he take any notice of us?'

Vera wasn't sure of the answer quite yet, but she knew all this would have to happen before she was discovered. A better hiding place was needed, and Vera knew the perfect spot.

SIX

ALMOST TWO HOURS HAD passed since Vera had gone to the paper shop and failed to return. And now it was a little short of an hour since Doris had dispatched Enid to look for her sister, instructing her to go as far as the paper shop and then to 'come straight back'.

It was as though Doris was attempting to pull together multiple strands of a complex piece of knitting and it was all unravelling in front of her. She had always admired her sister's mothering instincts. Annabelle had known what to do from the moment Enid was born. Or at least that was how it seemed to Doris. And when Vera came along, and Annabelle had to juggle the demands of a baby with the increasing demands of a five-year-old, she sailed through it all, while at the same time being a good wife to Matthew. Something had to give and in Doris's opinion Annabelle had let herself go. She was rarely out of her housecoat, rollers in her hair, a scarf covering them. The only time Doris had seen Annabelle wear lipstick was for the wedding of Doris to Bill. Whenever Doris raised the subject, which was rare, Annabelle would say she couldn't be doing with putting stuff on her face. Not even Pond's Cold Cream, which must be why she had so many lines and wrinkles, despite being barely two years older than Doris.

Yes, the girls were always clean and tidy, but Doris couldn't say as much for her sister's living conditions. The kitchen surfaces needed a good scrub, and there was no way of telling when the windows were last cleaned. Of course, the recent spate of bombings meant an extra layer of dust and grime over everything, but even during these war years Doris had kept to a strict cleaning regime. She prided herself on maintaining order. A neat and tidy house led to a neat and tidy life. That was Doris's motto, and it hadn't let her down yet. These last few days having Enid and Vera to stay had upset her routine. She loved them both, of course she did, but it was the unpredictability of children she couldn't tolerate. She couldn't help thinking that her sister had given them too much freedom. If Doris had children, she would be firm with them from the start, but there were no children and that suited Doris just fine.

For the first few years of their married life, it was as if she was holding her breath each month. A few times her period was late and when that happened Doris was gripped by fear. Their life would change irrevocably. Then her period started, and with it came relief. She and Bill had never spoken about it. But on the odd occasion they both visited Annabelle's house, Bill would return with a wistfulness about him for the rest of the day.

'Family, eh? That'll be us one day, love,' he said on one occasion.

Doris shrugged it off. She knew what he meant, even though he'd never come right out and ask her. Bill was what her father called 'a man's man'. No nonsense, straightforward.

And now she had taken responsibility for her sister's children and wished she hadn't. Nothing had been right since they arrived and, to set the seal on a disastrous twenty-four hours, both girls had gone off to who knew where. And it wasn't as if Bill could help. He had his own problems to sort out.

But Annabelle would be away for another day or more. Plenty of time for everything to be back to normal before her return. The alternative was unthinkable.

Doris would keep busy cleaning and tidying, maybe even a spot of baking. Perhaps try another batch of rock cakes, see if she couldn't get them to come out better than the last lot. The dried egg was never going to be as good as fresh, and the recipe called for more butter than she could justify using from their ration. But at least she had plenty of sugar. She kept the extra bag at the back of the larder, hidden behind the jars of preserves. Not that Bill would ever think to look in the larder. Cooking was women's work, as far as Bill was concerned.

Dried egg, the tiniest amount of butter, flour, sugar, baking powder, a handful of currants and a pinch of mixed spice, then a splash of milk and the mixture was ready. She always did the final mixing with her hand; she'd watched her mother do the same thing enough times. 'A light touch is what's needed,' her mother always said. 'They might be called rock cakes, but we don't want them to taste like rocks now, do we?'

Both of Doris's hands were covered in the sticky mixture when there was a bang on the door.

'Dear Lord, please don't let it be the police.'

A niggling thought that the local bobby would bring either of the girls back, reporting on some misdemeanour they had committed, hadn't been far from Doris's mind since the time they had been missing stretched from one hour to two and beyond.

She was loath to wipe her sticky hands down her apron, best to wash them under the kitchen tap with soap. The caller would have to wait. By the time she had dried her hands the banging on the door had become almost frenzied. But now it was accompanied by a voice. Not the police.

As Doris opened the front door her sister almost fell inside.

'Lord, Doris, I've been banging and banging. What took you so long?'

'Annabelle.'

So much to explain, questions to answer and little or no information that would be helpful to ease her sister's inevitable concern.

'I was baking. Why didn't you come round the back?'

They were both still hovering just inside the hallway.

'I thought the girls would answer the door, I wanted to surprise them.'

As Annabelle spoke, she moved away from her sister, heading towards the kitchen.

'Are they helping you with the baking? Enid's a dab hand when she puts her mind to it, but Vera... well, need I say more.'

Annabelle had arrived at the kitchen door, the scene of part-prepared rock cakes set out before her.

'Where are they? Don't tell me you've let them lounge about in their bedroom while you've been here cooking. At least they could be helping to wash up.'

Annabelle turned and moved past Doris to stand at the foot of the staircase.

'Enid, Vera, Mum's home.'

'They're not here. They're out,' Doris said, a flat tone to her voice.

'Why didn't you say so right away? Where's out?'

A moment's hesitation for Doris. Perhaps it was best to tell her sister everything, from the beginning. She rehearsed the phrases in her head. She imagined her sister's response. Why did you send Vera back out on her own? One question would lead to more and then the inevitable reprimand, taking Doris back to their own childhood when Annabelle was always in charge.

'Doris, has something happened? Tell me now and get it over with. I can see it written across your face.' Annabelle grabbed her sister's arm, forcing her to turn, until they stood facing each other, eye contact held steady, belying the tumult of emotion that would have been tangible for anyone walking into the kitchen at that moment.

'Like I said, they're out doing errands, but, yes, they've been gone a bit longer than I'd hoped. And you're back sooner than you thought. Everything alright?'

Annabelle wasn't going to be distracted. The time to talk about the whys and wherefores of her trip to Brighton would be after her children were safely back beside her.

'I'll put the kettle on, shall I?' Doris said, her voice rising in pitch as she struggled to sound calm.

'If you think I'm going to sit here supping tea while my girls are out who knows where, doing who knows what. I trusted you to watch over them, Doris. You've let me down.'

Annabelle stepped over the suitcase, which was still on the mat inside the front door and went out into the street. At the same moment the back door slammed, and Bill called out, 'It's sorted. I've settled it once and for all.'

SEVEN

JESSICA AND VERA MADE their way up Winchester Street, turning the corner into Sandy Close. At all times their gaze shifted left and right, ahead and behind; their focus was on reaching the haunted house without being discovered.

The weather was on their side. The streets were quiet. A fierce wind had whipped up a little after lunchtime, perhaps coinciding with the turn of the tide. Winchester Street was devoid of dog walkers and cyclists. Few had chosen to brave the strong north-easterly, just to stand in a queue for this week's rations. That could wait, perhaps Monday would bring more clement weather. There was always something in the store cupboard or larder that would suffice for supper.

And so their approach to the haunted house was clear. Jessica nodded at the chalk markings on the pavement, which had remained despite the showers of previous days.

'Mrs Cartwright gave me that chalk, you know. I didn't steal it,' Jesssica said.

'Then I'm sorry I called you a thief.' Vera paused, the beginnings of a frown across her forehead. 'Why did she give it to you?'

'I helped her carry a load of books from our classroom into that tearoom in Tensing Gardens. We did it one day in the holidays.'

'Why?'

'In case the school gets bombed, I suppose. Then we'll have to go there for our lessons.'

Thoughts of bombing raids were never far from Vera's mind, but she hadn't considered the school as a possible target. It was one place she felt safe, until now. Perhaps she wouldn't go back to school after this weekend. But where would she go? Living at Victoria Lodge without her mother was impossible to contemplate. Just spending that short time there this morning had proved that. The alternative – living with Auntie Doris – wasn't a much better option. And even that would only be possible if Auntie Doris hadn't run off with motorcycle man.

Vera and Jessica were still standing beside the hopscotch squares when they heard a whistle.

'Quick, let's hide.' Vera grabbed Jessica's hand and pulled her inside the porch of the Roebuck House. Or at least what remained of the porch. Originally brick built with a tiled roof, all that now remained was part of one of the walls, three rafters, jutting out from the main house with views of grey sky replacing the roof that once provided cover. It was hardly a hiding place.

The whistle again and then a face appearing through the thick privet hedge surrounding the garden.

'Thank goodness I've found you.' Enid's breathlessness was not just from running. 'What are you doing here? If Mum finds out, she'll kill you.'

'Is Mum home?' Vera said, receiving a shake of Enid's head by way of reply. A reprimand from her mother would be welcome. It would mean she had returned, although the fate of her father was still unknown.

'Jessica, you should know better than to bring Vera here. We've been told over and over not to come near the place.' Enid said.

'Because it's haunted.' Vera stated as a fact.

'No, because it's dangerous.' Enid emphasised her warning with a stamp of her foot. 'Look.' She pointed up at the remaining rafters, which were eaten away by woodworm and decayed by dry rot. 'And that's just the porch. Imagine what it's like inside.'

The opportunity to step inside was too good to miss. Vera was so close; she couldn't walk away now. Danger or no danger.

'You still haven't told me why you're here,' Enid said. 'And why is there a tea towel wrapped round your hand?'

'Motorcycle man,' Vera declared, as if that alone explained everything.

'What is she talking about?' Enid addressed her question to Jessica, who merely shrugged.

'Ask your sister.'

'There's a big secret I know about the man on the motorcycle – the one who nearly knocked us down – and Auntie Doris,' Vera said.

'What secret? Vera, we need to go back to Auntie Doris's house right now. You've been gone hours. She might even have called the police by now. And Vera, your hand. Have you hurt it?'

Vera's reply never came, as seconds later the air raid warning signal sounded. Vera's determination to step inside the haunted house now overrode any fears she had of being bombed, with Enid and Jessica swept along in the moment. All three tugged on the plank of wood that had been roughly nailed across the door. Moments later it gave way, and they were inside.

Only then was the true extent of the damage to the derelict property evident. Just one side of the hallway was intact. There was no door to the front room, merely a pile of rubble to step across. And once there they found nothing but broken furniture, among broken glass and timbers.

'We can't be in here, it's not safe,' Enid said. 'This is crazy, listen to that siren, do you want to get us all killed?'

'There'll be a hidey hole somewhere. Come on, help me find it.' Vera didn't wait for a response but led the way, along the hallway, to the back of the house, which seemed relatively unscathed from whatever catastrophe had befallen Roebuck House. It was much later the girls learned that the house hadn't taken a direct hit from a bombing raid in this war or any other. Instead, it had fallen into disrepair over decades. The windows providing target practice for the local lads, with damp eating away at the mortar, causing the brickwork to crumble away.

But once in the kitchen the scene they were presented with belied all they had seen to date. The kitchen was seemingly undisturbed by the decay affecting the rest of the building, walls, ceiling and windows all intact. In the centre of the kitchen stood a solid wooden table the surface scrubbed clean. At one end was an enamel plate, a part eaten chunk of bread remaining, and an enamel mug with the dregs of tea staining the bottom.

'Someone is living here,' Vera said. 'Look.' She held up the enamel mug for her sister and friend to see.

'Vera, this is not the time for you to start being a detective.' Not irritation, but a definite quiver in Enid's voice.

It seemed to Vera at that moment that it wasn't about choosing to be scared or choosing to be brave. The tower of fears that Vera had seen blocking her way just days ago, seemed to have vanished. In fact, it was as though she was on top of the tower, with a clear view forward. 'Come on, let's all get under the table and hold hands.'

And this time it was Enid who looked the most troubled when she said, 'I wish Mum was here'.

EIGHT

WITH EACH STEP ANNABELLE took from Doris's house her annoyance with her sister dissipated. Doris had voiced often enough that she struggled to understand children, they made her feel uncomfortable. Nevertheless, Annabelle had entrusted her girls to their aunt, certain there was little chance of a harmonious visit.

Her daughters were both strong in their own ways. Her youngest daughter craved the security that home offered, but despite Vera's fears Annabelle recognised a determination in her youngest daughter. A character trait that would see her through whatever life threw at her. Vera's endless questions were no more than the result of a lively mind, an inquisitive nature, an eagerness to learn and to understand. And, although she would never admit it, Annabelle felt an affinity with her youngest daughter, which she felt guilty about. It was wrong to have favourites. A mother's love must be shared equally. And so, by way of counterbalance, Annabelle was harder on Vera than she deserved.

The truth was that Annabelle at Vera's age had experienced all the confusion about life her daughter was trying to negotiate. Annabelle's own memories of schooldays were never far from her mind, years of being told off in class for her constant questions. It wasn't the done thing in those days. Children went to school to learn, and that meant listening to the teacher and only speaking when you were invited to. The comments in her school reports were a reminder.

'Annabelle would do well to listen more and talk less.'

'Annabelle is too inquisitive for her own good.'

And so, prevented from asking questions at school, she saved them up for when she got home. Often, she would burst into the kitchen straight after school with a question ready on her lips before she had even taken her coat off. Annabelle's father was always at work and so it fell to her mother to try to satisfy her daughter's thirst for knowledge. Vera's grandmother was not an educated woman, she rarely, if ever, picked up a book. Her talents lay in keeping a tidy home, being a good plain cook and making sure her daughters learned their manners. And so, Annabelle was left with her questions, just as Vera was now struggling with hers.

Standing on the front doorstep of Victoria Lodge, Annabelle took the key from her purse and unlocked the front door, stepping into the dark hallway.

'Vera, it's Mum.'

The need to feel her daughter's arms tucked tight around her waist was palpable. Seconds passed as she moved slowly from the hall through to the kitchen. An empty kitchen. Empty of people, but not of evidence. Biscuit crumbs scattered across the table, only the empty packet of Rich Tea fingers remaining, the wrapper tossed onto the draining board. Beside the wrapper an open tin of corned beef, the meat untouched. Annabelle picked up the tin and only then did she see the blood. Dark red spots on the sharp edge of the tin, where the blood had dried. More blood on the plate and spattered in the sink, the water diluting the scarlet red to muted shades of pink and palest rose.

'Oh Vera.' Her call this time more urgent. Her daughter was lying somewhere, losing blood. Perhaps she had fainted, unable to make it to a place of safety. Annabelle doubled over, cramps in her stomach a mixture of fear and anger. She had entrusted her daughters to Doris and her sister had let her down. She slid down onto one of the kitchen chairs, wrapping her arms around herself, trying to steady her nerves long enough to think straight. Where would Vera go to for help, if not to her aunt's?

Her daughter's friendship with Jessica Chandler was no secret. They'd got into numerous scrapes in the past, with Annabelle never certain if it was Jessica who led Vera astray, or the other way around.

Mrs Chandler answered Annabelle's knock within seconds.

'You've arrived just at the right moment. I've finished my bottling and decided I deserve a sit down with a cuppa and now you're here to join me.' Helen Chandler stepped back from the door, turning, anticipating Annabelle would follow her.

A strong smell of malt vinegar and pickling spices wafted through from the kitchen. It was a smell that would hang around for days. When Annabelle had done her own pickling the odour clung to carpets and curtains, such that Annabelle lost all appetite for the pickles themselves.

'I'm looking for Vera. I thought she might be here?'

The qualms in Annabelle's stomach, transferred to her voice. They started as a nervous fluttering, then travelled up into her chest where shallow breathing made it feel as though her lungs would explode.

'Vera isn't here,' Helen said, watching Annabelle look from left to right, as if by doing so her daughter would suddenly appear.

'And Jessica? Do you know when they last spoke to each other?'

It was only when Helen checked her watch that she realised her daughter had been gone for nearly an hour on what should have been no more than a ten-minute errand. She had been so absorbed in her pickling she had hardly given her daughter a thought.

'She's a dreamer that girl,' Helen said, and for a moment Annabelle was ready to rise to her daughter's defence. But then

Helen added, 'I gave Jessica a simple job to do. She should have been back ages ago. When did you last see Vera?'

There was no time to explain about Annabelle's journey to Brighton, about the blood she'd found, the fear that gripped her. 'I really need to find her.'

'There's no saying the two of them are together,' Helen said.

'If I see Jessica, I'll send her straight home.' Leaving Helen standing on her doorstep, Annabelle headed down Winchester Road.

As she walked Annabelle spoke quietly to herself, first listing the places where Vera might have gone to and rehearsing what she would say when she finally tracked her daughter down. It had to be 'when', not 'if'.

It was as she reached the junction of Winchester Road and Sandy Close that the air raid siren sounded. The few locals who were out, who moments before were going about their day, stopped still, as if a command had been issued by an army general. They turned in unison and headed towards the air raid shelter. The communal shelter had been built a little more than a year ago and word was that it could house no more than fifty people, but who was counting? At first a queue formed, but soon there was pushing and shoving to get in, an understandable need for haste, despite a recent report that one of the brick-built shelters on the other side of town had provided little comfort to the poor people inside. A nearby blast had shaken the walls, causing the concrete roof to fall in. Several people were badly injured, one of them still in hospital.

Once inside the shelter Annabelle nodded to several people she knew. There was little conversation, just half spoken mutterings of, 'Oh, not again,' and 'I wonder who will get it this time.'

Elderly men, not involved in fighting or the Home Guard, but left with their memories of the Great War, removed their jackets, gesturing to the women to sit.

Annabelle shook her head when offered a space beside Deirdre Ripton.

'I'd take the load off if I were you,' Deirdre said. 'Looks to me like you need to sit down before you fall down.'

Annabelle looked down at the area of floor that Deirdre was pointing to, but she wasn't seeing the floor and she wasn't listening to Deirdre's advice. She closed her eyes, picturing her youngest daughter who was terrified of air raids, and now with an injury that would leave her weak and even more afraid. Wherever she was now Annabelle was certain Vera would be almost hysterical.

'My Vera is missing,' Annabelle said, offering the words to anyone who might be listening.

'What do you mean, missing?' Deirdre said.

'I left her with my sister... I...' She couldn't finish the sentence because to do so would be to admit that just the day before she had abandoned her children. Stolen time away from being a mother and, as it turned out, away from being a wife.

When she had reached the guest house in Brighton where Matthew was due to meet her, the man on reception handed her a letter. A scribbled note from her husband explaining all leave had been cancelled, there was a crisis, he would explain when he next wrote. She should have returned home there and then. But there was such a temptation to enjoy the freedom, to walk along Brighton Pier, buy sixpenny worth of chips, covering them liberally with salt and vinegar before eating them while they were still hot enough to burn her tongue. It felt reckless, wicked.

She caught the eye of a passing stranger. He smiled, asked if he could sit beside her. They laughed at the seagulls squawking overhead. One swooped towards her and the man put his arm out, protecting her. After an hour or so the man took his leave, saying how much he had enjoyed her company. Not once did she mention she was a married woman, that her husband could be in danger at this very moment. She even hid her left hand so he wouldn't see her wedding ring.

Matthew had booked a double room in a charming guest house with a view of the sea. Annabelle stretched out on the double bed; joyful she hadn't had to launder the sheets. At breakfast the next morning she filled her plate with all that was on offer, freshly baked bread, home-made preserves tasting better than anything she had tasted before. And not once, in all the time she was away, did she give any real consideration to her daughters.

She had chosen to grab a few stolen hours and now she was being punished. Whatever might happen to Vera wasn't Jessica's fault, it wasn't Doris's fault, it was hers and hers alone.

'I saw your girls this morning,' a woman offered. 'They were in the queue at the greengrocer's. We were all after an orange or two but I'm pretty sure there were none left by the time they reached the top of the queue.'

Annabelle stared at the woman.

'I can't remember the last time I tasted an orange,' another woman said. 'Or a plate of freshly scrambled eggs.'

A few minutes passed when several people spoke of the food and drink they had been missing since the start of the fighting.

'I blame Chamberlain,' a man said.

'Not his fault, was it? At least he tried,' said another.

'The only person to blame is Hitler, him and his cronies,' a woman piped up. 'It's no good turning on our own, we have to pull together.'

The discussion continued, with some in agreement, while others shook their heads. Annabelle remained silent, barely listening to the debate. While her physical being was there in the shelter, her thoughts were immersed in a memory.

Her sixteenth birthday celebration. Her mother had made a cake and decorated it with sixteen candles. After they had eaten the sandwiches (neatly cut by Doris) and the strawberry junket (Annabelle's favourite) it was time to cut the cake.

'No, wait,' said her mother. 'You have to make a wish.'

All the party guests chanted in unison, 'Wish, wish, wish.'

Annabelle closed her eyes tight, made her wish and a second later blew out all the candles with one strong breath.

Everyone clapped and shouted hooray.

'Well, that didn't take long,' her mother said. 'You must have had the wish prepared.'

'It was easy,' Annabelle said. 'It's the same thing I've wished for for as long as I can remember.'

'Tell us then,' Doris said. 'If you don't tell us we won't believe you even made a wish.'

Before anyone could stop her, Annabelle declared, 'To marry a good man and have babies, of course. Two. One girl, one boy.'

'Boring,' Doris said, a hand covering her mouth as she pretended to yawn. 'Wouldn't you rather travel the world, or marry a millionaire?'

'Money will never buy you happiness, Doris,' their father said. 'Remember that.'

And now, in the darkness of the air raid shelter, Annabelle realised her mistake. Everyone knows for a wish to come true it has to stay secret. She'd been lucky so far; she did marry a good man. She had two children, right enough, although both daughters. And now there was every chance her luck had run out.

NINE

WHEN THE 'ALL CLEAR' sounded Vera was still gripping tightly to the hands of her friend and her sister. But it was as if she was reassuring them, rather than the other way around.

'Come on, we can move now. That's the all clear.' Jessica tugged her hand free of Vera's, shuffling back on her haunches until she was away from the table so that she could stand.

'I didn't hear any bombs land,' Enid said, following Jessica from their place of safety to stand beside her.

'Just because we didn't hear them doesn't mean they didn't land,' Vera said, not yet encouraged to leave her hiding place.

'They don't always drop bombs, at least sometimes they drop them once they're over the Channel. That way they only kill the fish,' Jessica said.

'But I like fish,' Vera said.

'You'll be for it,' Jessica said. 'Both of you.'

'Oh, and I suppose you won't?' Enid said. 'Weren't you supposed to be running an errand for your mum about an hour ago?' She gestured towards the empty basket that sat on the draining board.

'It's your sister's fault. She made me come here with her.'

While Jessica and Enid were arguing about who was to blame and why, Vera had crawled out from under the table. She continued to crawl to the kitchen doorway, then stood.

'Now where are you going?' Enid said.

'Ssh, I thought I heard something. Upstairs.'

She moved stealthily towards the wooden staircase and by the time she had reached the midway point Jessica and Enid were behind her.

'I don't think we should be doing this. These stairs don't look very safe.' Enid pointed down towards a split running across the full length of one of the stair treads, revealing a gap several inches wide. She stepped across it cautiously, following her sister who had reached the top, seemingly undeterred.

But then Vera stopped so sharply Jessica and Enid almost bumped into her.

'Watch out,' Jessica said, before gently manhandling Vera to one side to take the lead.

With no doors remaining to the first rooms they passed, light flooded through from the windows. Although the covering of dirt and grime made the light murky, giving rise to shadows as the girls moved along the landing.

A brief glance in each of the first two bedrooms revealed little of interest. Any bedroom furniture had been long since removed, the drag marks across the carpet, the deep indentations, the only remaining evidence of beds, dressing tables, wardrobes.

Reaching the far end of the landing they were faced with a closed door. Vera took charge. Wrapping her fingers around the doorknob, she twisted it, with no result.

'It's probably locked,' Enid said. 'Here, let me try.' This time, either because of Enid's technique or her strength, the door swung open.

'Wow,' said Jessica.

'Golly,' added Enid.

Only Vera was silent as she moved forward to inspect the contents of the room.

To the left, cardboard boxes, stacked from floor to ceiling. To the right, wooden crates filled with packets of varying sizes. Vera stepped forward, taking a packet and holding it up for the others to see. 'Granulated sugar,' she read. Putting that down she picked up another. 'Self-raising flour.'

'I don't understand. Why is someone keeping all these things here instead of in the shops?' Vera turned to the others, hoping for an explanation.

Now it was Jessica's turn to investigate. She moved across to the stack of boxes, pulled the lid open and removed another smaller box. 'Senior Service cigarettes,' she announced.

'They must be stolen,' Enid said with some authority. 'We'll need to report it to the police.'

'And get told off for being inside the haunted house?' Jessica said.

'What do you suggest then, clever clogs?' Enid said.

'We'll wait here to see if anyone comes to fetch one of the boxes. Then we'll know.' Vera said. A turnaround had occurred. Vera was no longer asking the questions; instead she was ready with answers.

'Oh, right, three silly girls confronting a criminal.' Enid said.

'He might have a gun. Robbers usually have guns, or heavy sticks they use to knock people over the head with.' Vera couldn't decide if she was scared or excited.

'Okay, that's enough.' It was time for Enid to take control. 'No one is going to knock us over the head or shoot us and that's because we're leaving right now, this minute. We should never have come here in the first place. Jessica, I blame you.'

'Hang on a minute. It was your sister who wanted to come. Everyone blames me when there's trouble, but it's never my fault.'

'I don't care about that now. I care about getting the three of us out of here without any more mishaps. Auntie Doris will have sent out a search party, so the police will probably be here any minute.'

The moment Enid finished speaking all three heard a noise coming from downstairs.

'It's a murderer, coming to kill us.' Vera stated it as fact.

'Ssh,' Enid put a finger to her lips. 'There's definitely someone moving about.'

Then footsteps on the stairs, followed by a shout. 'Who's there?' A man's voice, followed swiftly by the man himself.

A gasp of surprise came from Vera and Enid at the same moment. They knew this man. At least they recognised him. He was the same man who had nearly run them down, the same man Vera had seen kissing their Auntie Doris. Motorcycle man.

'What the heck...' The man towered above them, his head almost touching the slope of the ceiling. 'You shouldn't be here. How did you get in anyway and what do you think you're doing poking your nose into other people's business? You'd better scarper before I lose my temper.'

It was the youngest among them who was the first to speak.

'I bet these things don't belong to you.' Vera's voice was defiant.

'Like I said, it's none of your business.' The man grabbed the packet of cigarettes from Jessica's hand, returning it to the box and closing the lid. 'Do your folks know you're here?'

Watching the man holding his motorcycle helmet in the crook of his arm, Jessica offered up a comment that risked giving the game away.

'Are you the man who is *friendly* with Vera's Auntie Doris?' Her inference didn't go unnoticed by anyone in the room.

'Doris? You're her niece, are you?'

'I'm Vera, she's Enid. We're sisters and you know our aunt. I've seen you... together. And now Uncle Bill is home you'll be for it,' Vera added. 'You might be tall, but my Uncle Bill is really strong. He's a soldier and he'll punch you on the nose, you see if he doesn't.'

There was a moment when Enid was staring first at Vera, then at the man, wondering what her sister was talking about. And then the most unexpected reaction of all. The man dropped his motorcycle helmet to the floor and began to laugh. A great big guffawing laugh that saw him doubling over and then straightening up again. The laughter only stopped when he started to cough. He took a packet of cigarettes from the top pocket of his leather jacket and lit one.

'You're funny, you know. Very funny. And gutsy too. A credit to the family,' he said.

'What do you mean?' Vera said.

'We're related, aren't we? We're family.' At this the man started laughing again, between taking drags on his cigarette. 'It's very nice to meet you both – Vera and Enid – that's right, isn't it?' He looked from one girl to the other and then, 'Shame we've never been properly introduced. Not even a photograph. And you,' he looked over at Jessica, 'I guess you're the outsider, so to speak?'

'You're the outsider,' Vera said. 'How dare you pretend you're related to us. We don't even know who you are and if you don't know us, that's proof.'

'Pipe down, young madam and I'll tell you.'

But before the story could be told, a shout brought all in the upstairs room to silence.

'Vera, Enid, are you in here?'

'It's Mum.' Vera's shriek was followed by her swift departure along the landing and down the stairs, with Enid, then Jessica, then 'motorcycle man' close behind.

TEN

VERA HURLED HERSELF INTO her mother's outstretched arms, pressing her face into her chest. Her account of the events of the last twenty-four hours spilling out, not only garbled, but muffled too.

'Oh, Vera, we've been so worried about you. What are you doing here? And Enid, you should know better.' Annabelle's reprimand to her eldest daughter came out sharper than she intended. To compensate she held an arm out to Enid, pulling her into a hug beside her little sister. 'There now. The important thing is that you're both safe. And Jessica, you'd best go straight home and put your mother's mind at rest.'

The bystander overseeing the reunion had until this moment said nothing. He chose this moment to speak.

'Don't you all make for a cosy family.'

At that, Annabelle turned her attention to the man, eyeing him cautiously, questions hovering on her lips, the first being, 'And who might you be and why are you here with my girls?'

The man gave a hollow laugh. 'I'll tell you who I might be. In fact, I'll tell you who I am. I'm family, that's what.'

'Whose family?'

'Yours. Or at least your brother-in-law's.'

'Bill? How are you related to Bill? And how is it I've never heard of you?'

'I'm his brother. The black sheep turned prodigal. The one no one wants to talk about who's turned up with treats a-plenty to tempt you with.'

Vera wasn't listening, she had lost all interest in motorcycle man. She had only one question.

'Is Dad dead?' Three words that stilled the group who were standing close together at the foot of the staircase.

'Oh darling, no your dad's not dead. What on earth made you think that?'

'We saw the newspaper,' Vera said. 'It said an RAF plane had been shot down and we thought...'

'I'd suddenly up and left you both because I'd had bad news?'

'Something like that.' Vera pulled out from her mother's embrace and looked down at the floor. 'Is Dad hurt?'

'Your dad is just fine, and he sends you both big hugs and lots of love.' The truth of Annabelle's stolen moments of freedom couldn't be shared, not now, probably not ever.

'I cut my hand.' Vera held up her left hand still wrapped in the teacloth.

Annabelle pulled her daughter close again. 'I know, I saw the blood. I was so scared for you, darling. You must have been scared too.'

This wasn't the time for Vera to explain how it was that the fears that once were overwhelming her had somehow altered into something else entirely. And even if it was the time she couldn't have explained it.

'Right, seeing as how none of you are interested in getting to know a new relation, I'll take my leave and say goodbye.' The man pushed past Annabelle.

'I'll be seeing my sister shortly. Then I'll hear the truth of it,' Annabelle said.

'Ah, the lovely Doris,' the man winked. 'Well, you might hear the truth and you might not.' And with that the man was gone.

Annabelle held tightly to the hands of both daughters as they walked the short distance to Doris's house.

'Mum, I know a secret. About that man and Auntie Doris.'

Vera's statement brought their walking to a halt.

'What kind of a secret? Vera, it's one thing to enjoy a spot of make-believe, but you mustn't make up stories about anyone in the family. That's not make-believe, it's lying.'

'I'm not lying, Mum. Really. I saw them together and then Auntie Doris kissed the man and got into his motorcycle sidecar and they went off together.'

'When? When did you see this?'

'Uncle Bill was away fighting and then he came home suddenly, and he and Auntie Doris looked very grumpy at breakfast,' Vera said.

'Why didn't you tell me about it?' Enid said. 'You told Jessica and you didn't tell me, your own sister.'

Vera couldn't quite decide why she hadn't shared the secret with Enid. Perhaps it was something to do with being grown up. Most of the time grown-ups dealt with problems on their own, worked out ways of sorting them out and sometimes never talked about them. Maybe that's what being grown up meant.

'We'll hear no more of it just now. We'll go back to Doris's and fetch your things. And you're not to say a word about this man, do you hear?'

'But Mum...' Vera was determined to have the last word.

'No, Vera. You heard me.'

'Mum, there's something else. I think motorcycle man is living in Roebuck House and storing loads of stuff there, hundreds and hundreds of cigarettes and more packets of sugar than anyone could use in a whole year.' Vera tugged at her mother's arm to add emphasis to her words.

But her mother wasn't listening. At least that's how it seemed to Vera.

Back at Doris's house, with the girls' belongings gathered and thanks offered that could hardly be described as whole-hearted, they took their leave.

'I'll pop back to see you in an hour or so,' was Annabelle's parting remark.

Back at Victoria Lodge, the bloodied scene Vera had left remained unchanged. Enid was instructed to boil a kettle. 'There's some disinfectant under the kitchen sink. Give everything a good wipe round, then throw the cloth away. I'll see to your sister; we need to make sure the cut isn't infected.'

She led Vera to the sink, turned on the cold tap and held her daughter's hand under the flowing water.

'Ouch.'

'Hold still now.'

'But it hurts.'

'Don't be a baby. Enid, pass me that disinfectant, will you?'

'Ouch, it stings.'

Annabelle wiped the wound dry, ignoring her daughter's protestations. Taking a clean bandage from the dresser drawer she wrapped it tightly around Vera's hand.

'It's too tight, I can't breathe.'

'Now you're being silly. Having a bandage around your hand isn't going to stop you breathing. We'll leave it like that until I get back from Doris's, then I'll take another look at it.'

'Are you going to ask Auntie Doris about kissing that hairy man?' Vera said.

Enid giggled, receiving a disapproving frown from her mother.

'That's not for you to worry about. On the way back I'll stop at the grocer's, see if I can't get us something nice for our tea.'

The mention of food reminded Vera of her hunger pangs; the soreness from the cut on her hand forgotten.

'I'm starving,' she said. Before her mother could respond with the usual reply, Vera followed up with, 'I really am starving. I've had no food since...'

'Since you ate a whole packet of biscuits from the emergency store,' Enid said, holding out the empty biscuit wrapper from the rubbish bin.

'Exactly.'

ELEVEN

A FEW MINUTES LATER Annabelle left the girls with strict instructions not to step outside the house, not even to go into the garden.

The short walk to her sister's house was barely enough time to prepare her thoughts. What right did she have to question her sister, when not hours ago she was herself enjoying the attentions of a stranger. The very act of challenging Doris would be seen as hypocritical if her sister knew the truth.

Regardless, any plans Annabelle had for a discreet conversation with Doris were dismissed when she was greeted at the front door by her sister's husband.

'Bill.'

'Doris is out back, scrubbing the stove. You can always tell when she's upset. She's been at it since you left. Your girls alright now? Sounds like they gave you both a fright. Good job you came back early, eh? Matthew alright, is he?'

'Thanks Bill. Yes.' She felt like a naughty schoolgirl who had been caught out by the teacher.

In the kitchen her sister was kneeling on the floor, her head almost inside the oven as she stretched to reach the back with a scouring pad. Annabelle gave a little cough to announce her arrival, but her sister continued with her cleaning.

'Doris, stop that a minute. I need to talk to you.' Annabelle tapped her sister on the back, causing her to move so sharply she almost banged her head on the oven roof.

'Goodness, you gave me a fright.' She twisted around, kneeling and looking up at her sister. 'Annabelle, I'm sorry, really I am. I thought I could do it, but well... there's a reason I don't have children. I like my routine and I'm not ashamed to admit it.'

'That's not all you like.' Annabelle's voice dropped to a whisper.

'And what is that supposed to mean?' There was nothing quiet or conciliatory about Doris's tone. 'Are you saying it's my fault your precious Vera doesn't know how to behave herself?'

'What's all the shouting about?' Bill pushed open the kitchen door and looked from his wife to his sister-in-law and back again.

'I just need a quiet word with my sister.' Annabelle said at last.

'There's nothing you can't say in front of Bill.' Doris stood, moving to her husband's side. Her face was flushed and with her pink rubber gloves still on, a patterned scarf around her hair and her floral apron tied neatly around her waist, she reminded Annabelle of a garden bursting with riotous colour.

'Well, this is private,' Annabelle said. 'It's... about women's things.'

'In that case, I'm off,' Bill grabbed his jacket from the kitchen chair, then, directing his gaze at his wife, he said, 'And this time I'll make sure it's sorted once and for all.'

Doris's only response was a surreptitious nod. Once Bill had pulled the kitchen door closed, she said, 'What's this about women's things? You're not going to tell me you're in the family way again, are you? Your Matthew's been gone for months.'

'It's nothing of the sort. I said that to get your Bill out of the way.' Annabelle paused. 'Doris, I'm going to ask you a question and I need you to tell me the truth. Do you promise?'

'Now what?'

But Annabelle no longer had her sister's attention. Bill had departed, and in his place stood Enid and Vera, Enid grasping something small in her hand.

'I told you girls not to leave the house, what are you doing here?' Annabelle said.

'There's a telegram.' Enid thrust the envelope into her mother's hand.

'Dad's dead, isn't he? That's why they've sent the telegram.' Vera sidled over to her mother, grabbing the hand holding the telegram.

Annabelle looked first at her youngest daughter and then at the telegram.

'You'd best sit down.' Doris guided her sister towards a chair, Vera still attached like a limpet to her mother's arm.

'Aren't you going to open it, Mum,' Enid said. The expression on her mother's face seemed at that moment to be more terrifying than the possible contents of the telegram.

Annabelle gently prised Vera's fingers from her arm, giving a forced smile, which left her face as soon as it arrived. Then Annabelle slid her finger under the envelope flap, pulling out the small, folded sheet.

The others in the room fixed their gaze on Annabelle's face, as if her expression alone would confirm the contents of the telegram.

Annabelle scanned the words, remaining silent. She handed the telegram to Doris, rose from the chair and went out the back door, pulling it firmly closed behind her.

It was left to Doris to inform her nieces their father was 'Missing in action'.

'What does it mean?' Vera as always craved explanation, clarification. 'If they can't find Dad, they must be looking in the wrong places.'

Enid put her arm around her sister, pulling her close. 'It's what they say when they think someone's been killed but they can't find the body.'

'That's not true,' Doris's voice was firm. 'There are all sorts of reasons someone might be missing in action. His plane might have had a problem and he might have parachuted out. He might have landed in France and been taken in by a nice French family. You'll see, your dad is just fine, I'm sure of it.'

'You don't know that.' Vera pulled away from her sister and ran to the back door.

'Your mum wants to be on her own just now, Vera.' Doris tugged Vera back from opening the door.

'I want Mum.' A shriek this time, followed by tears that came quietly at first and then more loudly. Her bravery of just hours ago had somehow seeped away at the very moment the telegram boy thrust the envelope into her sister's hand.

'Ssh now.' Doris had been left to deal with a situation she felt ill-equipped to deal with. She was sorry for her sister, of course she was, but...Annabelle was a mother, skilled in these matters and Doris was what? An aunt, yes, but an aunt who had chosen a different path, away from emotional responsibilities, towards practicality and order. Telling the girls to stay put Doris went into the back garden to find Annabelle sitting on a dry patch of grass. She was slumped forward, her head over her knees.

'You'd best come in. Your girls need you.'

Annabelle looked up, wiping her face, which was wet from tears and now smudged with grass stains. 'You've always thought me a good mother, haven't you?' She stood, face to face with her sister. 'A good mother and a good wife, even if I don't have a tidy house. That's what you think, isn't it? But it's not true.' Her voice rose in pitch. 'It's a lie, all of it. I'm not a good mother, I'm not even a good wife. And now all I can hope to be is a good widow.'

'Of course you're a good mother and a good wife to Matthew. You're hysterical, Annabelle. You don't know what you're saying.'

'Let he who is without sin cast the first stone. That's what they say, isn't it? Well, there will be no stones cast here. Not today.'

Hours later Annabelle lay in bed, Enid to one side of her, Vera the other. The same silent question was being asked by each of them. 'Why?' A question asked across the country, across Europe and before long across the world.

TWELVE

A WEEK PASSED BEFORE there was any further news. Each time Annabelle saw the telegram boy cycling down any of the streets in Tamarisk Bay her heart began to thud such that her breathing became laboured. She watched as the boy knocked on someone else's door and felt a wave of relief, soon followed by guilt. Not her husband, but someone else's, or perhaps a brother or son.

Every day the newspapers reported terrible losses. The German forces were advancing through France. Until now parts of France were safe in the designated 'free zone', but how long that would last only God knew. And how long before an invasion of Britain. Tamarisk Bay was there on the south coast, the first line of defence.

Sleepless nights saw Annabelle tossing and turning, haunted by images of German tanks parading down the seafront of Tamarisk Bay, swastika flags hanging from the Town Hall. Several times she woke calling out, only to find Enid kneeling beside her bed comforting her.

'Ssh Mum, you're having a bad dream.' Her eldest daughter protecting her, when it should have been the other way around.

Annabelle stayed away from her sister's house for three days, unable to rationalise her opinions about her sister's behaviour.

Doris was an adult; she was entitled to make her own mistakes. It was really none of Annabelle's business. More than that, who was she to pass judgement?

But then she found herself knocking on her sister's front door.

'Annabelle.' Doris pulled her inside. 'Is there news?'

Annabelle shook her head, following her sister into the kitchen, watching her as she filled the kettle and put it on the stove.

'Where's Bill?'

'Gone back to his barracks. God knows when I'll see him again. They never know when they're going to get leave. But I don't need to tell you that.'

'Every minute I'm expecting another telegram, but so far...' Annabelle's voice tailed off.

'Poor you. I can just imagine...'

'But that's not why I'm here.' The moment had come and yet Annabelle was uncertain how to proceed. She was relying on Vera having told her the truth about what she had seen. Vera wasn't a liar but there had been occasions when her imagination had overtaken her sense of reality.

'Does Bill have a brother?' Now the words were out, the rest of her questions didn't feel so daunting.

Doris gave a slow nod as if calculating her response. After a moment's pause, she said, 'Why?'

'Why doesn't matter so much just now. Does he, or doesn't he?'

'Bill doesn't like people knowing. His brother hasn't always been on the right side of the law... if you get my drift.'

'He's been in prison?'

'Well, no, at least not yet.' Doris sat, landing heavily on the kitchen chair as if relieved of a great weight. 'He's not a bad chap though. Not really.' She spoke as if she was trying to convince herself as much as her sister.

'Doris, are you over-friendly with Bill's brother?'

Doris stood, flicking her hair back and smoothing it down. The utilitarian garments she had been wearing when Annabelle last visited, when she had been fervently cleaning the oven, were now replaced with a smart A-line navy skirt, a blouse with a small polka dot pattern to it, a bow tied neatly at the neckline. She turned her back on her sister and wandered over to the kitchen sink, looking out over the back garden.

'Like I said, he's not a bad chap, he makes me laugh, and he's quite the charmer.' Her voice softened and Annabelle sensed she was smiling as she spoke.

'And Bill knows, does he?'

Doris turned sharply, a flush rising on her face.

'He knows you like this brother of his more than you should?'

'There's nothing wrong with being kind to relatives. Family must stick together. You can't disagree with that.'

'What's his name, this brother?'

'Jonathan.'

'Did you know Jonathan is storing goods in the derelict house at the end of Sandy Close. And not just any old goods. Doris, is Jonathan selling stuff on the black market?'

'Oh, it's all a fuss about nothing. He managed to get his hands on a few things and he's able to make a living by selling them off. There are plenty of folks who are only too happy if they can get hold of an extra bag of sugar. Aren't you sick of all this rationing? I know I am.'

'And you'll visit him when he's been sent to prison, will you? He could get years.'

'Bill has seen to it.'

'Seen to it, how?'

'I don't know, I didn't ask.' Doris was defiant. 'And yes, perhaps I did get over friendly with him. Bill was away and if you must know, I was missing male company. Are you so perfect you've never put a step wrong?'

And there it was, the spectre of Annabelle's guilt laid bare.

'How did you know? About Jonathan and me?' Doris asked.

'Vera.'

'Aah.'

'And he's gone now, has he?'

'Like I said, Bill sorted it out before he went back to base.'

There was little more to be said. The sisters embraced, Annabelle promising to get in touch the moment there was news. And then, before leaving, she clasped her sister's hand. 'The punishment doesn't always fit the crime, does it? But whether it fits or not, we are always punished, one way or another.' Could fate really be so cruel as to punish her daughters too? She would be a widow, but they would be fatherless, when they had done nothing wrong, and her only crime was grabbing those few sweet hours of freedom.

It was Wednesday, early evening, when the next air raid came. The Stubbs family took refuge in the understairs cupboard. Annabelle sang without any prompting from Vera and soon both girls joined in, continuing until the all clear was sounded.

By Friday new glass had been fitted into the broken window, so that Enid could move back into her bedroom and Vera could write another story, undisturbed. Later that week the tale of the singing gained Vera a gold star from Mrs Cartwright, who asked Vera to read the story out to the whole class.

Annabelle succeeded in quelling her daughter's inquisitiveness about 'motorcycle man' by providing as few details about Jonathan Frith as possible. The man was Uncle Bill's brother and Auntie Doris was being friendly, just as you should be with a brother-in-law. And now the man had gone away, moved on to another town.

'So, we won't be seeing him again? And all those boxes of stuff, has he taken it all with him?' Vera asked.

'He was looking after them for someone, that's all.' Annabelle risked a white lie to bring Vera's questioning to an end, at least for now.

'There's so much I don't understand, Mum,' Vera said, her sighing making Annabelle smile. 'I guess I'll have to wait until I'm grown up before I know all the answers.'

'Trust me, darling, even grown-ups don't have all the answers.'

That evening Annabelle sat on the edge of Vera's bed, leaning over to kiss her goodnight. As she did a book fell from the bedside table onto the floor.

'What's this? *The Secret Garden.* Do you know your aunt and I used to take it in turns to read this book when we were young.'

'I know. Auntie Doris said I could borrow it, as long as I looked after it. I started reading it that Friday...'

'The Friday I went away.'

'I was so scared, Mum. I thought you would never come home and that we would have to live with Auntie Doris forever. And then I realised that I could choose to be scared, or I could choose not to be scared.'

Annabelle had made a choice too. Just days ago she had chosen to turn her back on her responsibilities as a wife and mother. For a few hours of freedom. Her sister, Doris, had chosen to risk her marriage for the sake of a flirtation with a man who himself had chosen to challenge the law for his own benefit. Each decision led to a path, that in itself could lead to a destructive dead end, or could lead to a roundabout that provided a route back to safety.

Annabelle took her daughter's hand, clasping it in hers. 'You chose to be brave. Enid told me how you led them into a safe place when the air raid siren went off.'

'But I went into the very place you had told me not to go.'

'You made a judgement and it was a good judgement and for that I'm very proud of you.'

'So, I can go and play hopscotch down Sandy Close again?'

'You can, but only if you promise me not to go inside Roebuck House again.'

'Because it really is haunted?'

'Because it's dangerous. You saw that for yourself. I don't want you coming home with a broken head, do I? Think of the fuss you made over that little scratch on your hand.'

The scratch was now referred to as Vera's 'corned beef cut.' It had healed well but had been a useful excuse for Vera not to get too involved in daily chores. Each time washing up or laying the table was mentioned Vera held her hand up, a look of dismay on her face. 'My hand hurts.'

'And I think it's time you took on your share of the chores again, don't you?' Annabelle said with a wink. 'Now settle down and sleep and we'll wait to see what tomorrow will bring.'

On the first Saturday after Annabelle's visit to her sister, the telegram boy knocked at the door of Victoria Lodge. Annabelle called her daughters in from the back garden where they had been playing catch. The three of them sat to one side of the kitchen table and held hands. Then Enid nodded to her mother, before letting her hand go, freeing her up to open the telegram.

Annabelle read the words aloud, her voice breaking before she uttered the final syllable.

'Corporal Matthew Stubbs confirmed safe and well.'

And then it was hugs and whispered words of 'Thank you, dear God,' from Enid, 'Hooray' from Vera. No words from Annabelle, just tears pricking at her eyes.

'Will Dad come home now?' Vera said, before doing a hop and skip around the kitchen table.

'Soon, my darling, very soon.'

'Then Dad and I will go down to Bottle Alley and even though we can't eat sweets yet, Dad can tell me the story about the Everton mint. Because sweets aren't important, are they, it's being together that matters, isn't it, Mum?'

'Yes, darling, that really is all that matters.'

ABOUT BOTTLE ALLEY

FOR REGULAR READERS OF my Sussex Crime novels and novellas you will know that the seaside town of Tamarisk Bay is modelled on my own hometown of St Leonards-on-Sea in East Sussex. St Leonards-on-Sea nestles in-between Hastings to the east and Bexhill-on-Sea to the west.

In Choices we are told about one of Vera's favourite places. Before the war she and her father often visited Bottle Alley, sitting together on the concrete seats, looking out to sea, while Matthew Stubbs recounted stories of happy times to his young daughter. And it is Bottle Alley that Vera longs to return to, as soon as the war is over and her father is back home with the family.

So, I was delighted to be able to share a photo of Bottle Alley with you, by way of the cover image for this book. And here is a brief background to its history...

Bottle Alley was the brainchild of the 'concrete' king of Hastings - one Sidney Little. Back in the early 1930s Little came up with a plan to create a covered walkway some half a mile long, stretching from St Leonards-on-Sea through to Hastings. It seems that Little was a pioneer when it came to recycling, coming up with the idea of reusing old tramway granite setts to face the walls to take the full force of the sea. After a short delay for funds to be raised, construction began in earnest and the walkway was opened on 12 May 1934 by the Marquis of Reading.

The original construction involved glass shutters covering the openings, offering even more protection from the weather, giving the local residents a chance to stroll along the promenade on the wettest of days. Little's other idea was to face the concrete walls with small pieces of reclaimed coloured glass - giving the walkway the name 'Bottle Alley'.

Today the glass shutters are no longer in place, but that doesn't deter the many locals and visitors to the town to enjoy the place. What's more, in 2017, coloured lights were installed along the full length of Bottle Alley, providing an opportunity for beautiful evening light shows, spilling out across the sea.

Thanks to the following for the information provided here:
https://www.hastings.gov.uk/arts-culture/bottle/
https://www.1066.net/bottlealley/
https://historymap.info/Bottle_Alley

ABOUT THE SUSSEX CRIME SERIES

THE SUSSEX CRIME SERIES of novellas recount the stories of several of the characters from the Sussex Crime series of novels. The novellas are all set earlier in the lives of the characters, giving readers the chance to discover more about the experiences that brought them to the point where we meet them in the first novel of the series: The Tapestry Bag.

If you enjoyed this novella, take a look at the other short reads in this series:

DIVIDED WE FALL - 1st in the series
MORE THAN ASHES - 2nd in the series
WAITING FOR SUNSHINE - 3rd in the series
THE HARVEST - 4th in the series

If you are new to Isabella Muir's Sussex Crime series and you would like to read more then look out for the full-length novels in the series:

THE SUSSEX MYSTERY SERIES
Featuring young librarian and amateur sleuth - Janie Juke
BOOK 1: THE TAPESTRY BAG*
BOOK 2: LOST PROPERTY*
BOOK 3: THE INVISIBLE CASE*
*Also available as an audiobook

As a reader your words make all the difference

Honest reviews of my books help other readers find them. As an independent author I don't have the backing of a publisher or a team of publicists. I can't advertise in the traditional way, but I do have one thing going for me, and that's a group of engaged readers. If you enjoyed this book I would be very grateful if you could spend just five minutes leaving a review (as short as you like) on Goodreads or your favourite online book review websites, book groups, your own blogs and social media sites.

Thank you!
www.isabellamuir.com

ABOUT THE AUTHOR

Isabella is never happier than when she is immersing herself in the sights, sounds and experiences of family life in Sussex from the Second World War through to the 1960s. Researching all aspects of family life back then formed the perfect launch pad for her works of fiction. Isabella rediscovered her love of writing fiction during two happy years working on and completing her MA in Professional Writing with Falmouth University and since then she has gone on to publish six novels, five novellas and two short story collections.

Her love of Italy shines through all her work and, as she is half-Italian, she has enjoyed bringing all her crime novels to an Italian audience with Italian translations, which are very well received.

Her latest novel, *After the Storm,* is the second novel in a new series of *Sussex Crimes,* featuring retired Italian detective, Giuseppe Bianchi who is escaping from tragedy in Rome, only to arrive in the quiet seaside town of Bexhill-on-Sea, East Sussex, to come face-to-face with it once more.

Her first *Sussex Crime Mystery* series features young librarian and amateur sleuth, Janie Juke. Set in the late 1960s, in the fictional seaside town of Tamarisk Bay, we meet Janie, who looks after the mobile library. She is an avid lover of Agatha Christie stories – in particular Hercule Poirot. Janie uses all she has learned from the Queen of Crime to help solve crimes and mysteries. As well as three novels, there are three novellas in the series, which explore some of the back story to the Tamarisk Bay characters.

Isabella's standalone novel, *The Forgotten Children*, deals with the emotive subject of the child migrants who were sent to Australia – again focusing on family life in the 1960s, when the child migrant policy was still in force.

Find out more by visiting: www.isabellamuir.com

BY THE SAME AUTHOR

BRAND NEW SUSSEX MYSTERY SERIES!

Featuring retired Italian detective - Giuseppe Bianchi

CROSSING THE LINE *

AFTER THE STORM *

THE SUSSEX MYSTERY SERIES

Featuring young librarian and amateur sleuth - Janie Juke

BOOK 1: THE TAPESTRY BAG *

BOOK 2: LOST PROPERTY *

BOOK 3: THE INVISIBLE CASE *

THE SUSSEX CRIME MYSTERIES

A Janie Juke trilogy - box set

SUSSEX MYSTERY NOVELLAS

Featuring characters from the Janie Juke novels

DIVIDED WE FALL

MORE THAN ASHES

WAITING FOR SUNSHINE

THE HARVEST

CHOICES

THE FORGOTTEN CHILDREN *

A story about a mother's search for her child

TWELVE AT CHRISTMAS

An anthology of twelve Christmas-themed short stories

IVORY VELLUM

An anthology of short stories

*Also available as an audiobook.

www.isabellamuir.com

www.ingramcontent.com/pod-product-compliance
Lightning Source LLC
Chambersburg PA
CBHW030843200726
48285CB00007B/2530